Don't Chicken Out

NOT-SO-
ORDINARY
GIRL

Don't Chicken Out

Shawn K. Stout

Illustrated by Victoria Ying

Aladdin
New York   London   Toronto   Sydney   New Delhi

ALADDIN

An imprint of Simon & Schuster Children's Publishing Division

1230 Avenue of the Americas, New York, NY 10020

First Aladdin paperback edition May 2013

Text copyright © 2013 by Shawn K. Stout

Illustrations copyright © 2013 by Victoria Ying

All rights reserved, including the right of reproduction in whole or in part in any form.

ALADDIN is a trademark of Simon & Schuster, Inc.,

and related logo is a registered trademark of Simon & Schuster, Inc.

Also available in an Aladdin hardcover edition.

For information about special discounts for bulk purchases,

please contact Simon & Schuster Special Sales at 1-866-506-1949 or

business@simonandschuster.com.

The Simon & Schuster Speakers Bureau can bring authors to your live event.

For more information or to book an event contact the Simon & Schuster Speakers Bureau at

1-866-248-3049 or visit our website at www.simonspeakers.com.

Designed by Jessica Handelman

The text of this book was set in Perpetua Std.

Manufactured in the United States of America 0414 OFF

2 4 6 8 10 9 7 5 3

Library of Congress Control Number: 2012953812

ISBN 978-1-4169-7111-5 (pbk)

ISBN 978-1-4169-7929-6 (hc)

ISBN 978-1-4424-3499-8 (eBook)

For Rosie

• Chapter 1 •

Fiona Finkelstein was flat-out tired. Talking to grown-ups always made her that way. Especially when their answer was NO SIRREE BOB, NO WAY JOSÉ, NOT ON YOUR LIFE YOUNG LADY. That was their answer a lot of the time lately.

It wasn't the "no" by itself that was so bad. It was all of the other stuff that always and forever came along with it.

For example, just this morning, when Fiona asked her dad if they could get a real live monkey named Mr. Funbucket that she could keep in her room, Dad didn't just say no. He went on and on forever and ever about how monkeys are not pets and how they belong in the jungle and how speaking of jungles, had she cleaned her mess of a room yet? But what she wanted to know was, why did everything have to do with her mess of a room?

Even when she pointed this out, Dad said, "Well, if you cleaned your room more often, maybe we wouldn't have to talk about it all the time."

"*Then* could I get a monkey?"

"Not a chance," he said.

At school there were more nos.

"Can we take a field trip to California?" Fiona asked her teacher, Mr. Bland. They had just started talking about the California gold rush in social studies when Fiona brought it up.

"Sure," said Mr. Bland. "We can leave tomorrow." Only, he didn't say it in a Fiona-you're-a-genius-that's-the-best-idea-I've-ever-heard kind of way.

"Oh, Boise Idaho!" said Harold Chutney, who apparently didn't get that what Mr. Bland was really saying was N-O.

"He's being sarcastic," said Milo Bridgewater. "There's no way they'd let us go to California for school."

"Can we please get back to the gold rush?" said Mr. Bland. "If you don't mind."

Milo raised his hand and said, "How come we don't ever get to go anywhere? In my old school in Minnesota, we used to go to the park and to the lake all the time."

This isn't Minnesota, Fiona wanted to say out loud. *This is Ordinary, Maryland. And nothing much happens in Ordinary.*

Mr. Bland puffed out his cheeks as the mean words started filling up his mouth. Here's the thing about mean words: They want to get out. But Mr. Bland's lips must have been pretty strong, because he kept those words inside until he was able to swallow them down. And when all the puffiness left his cheeks, he cleared his throat. Then he said, "As a matter of fact, we are going somewhere."

The whole class shouted "Where?" at the same time. Fiona gripped the sides of her desk and waited.

Mr. Bland smiled and said real slow, on account of the fact that he liked kids to suffer, "To. The. Great. Ordinary. Fair."

Fiona let go of her desk. She folded her arms across her chest. That wasn't even close to California.

Everybody else must have noticed that too, because there was a lot of moaning and huffing from all sides. Mr. Bland said, "I guess nobody wants to hear about your part in this year's fair."

"I do," said Milo.

Everybody quieted down after that, and Mr. Bland said, "Every year our school participates in the Great Ordinary Fair in some way or another. It's a nice way to be a part of our community."

"That might be fun," said Milo, looking at Fiona for approval.

Fiona chewed on her Thinking Pencil. The fair might not be a trip to California, but it could still be okay, as long as they could be in charge of games or rides or even parking. Anything except . . .

"Maps," said Mr. Bland. "Our class is in charge of handing out maps."

Fiona moaned. "Not maps! Maps are just as bad

as tearing tickets." Which is what she'd had to do at last year's fair. Oh boy, the paper cuts.

"I don't want to hear any complaints," said Mr. Bland.

"I like maps," said Harold.

"Not these kind you don't," said Fiona. "These aren't treasure maps, you know."

Harold plugged his nose with his finger in a pout. "Oh."

"What about parking attendants?" asked Fiona. "Could some of us maybe be parking attendants instead?"

"Mrs. Weintraub's fifth grade has that covered," he said.

"No fair."

"Enough," said Mr. Bland. "Now back to the gold rush."

In the cafeteria, Fiona's mind was stuck in California. How she could get there. How she could see her mom again. Fiona's mom was an actress in California, and lately Fiona saw her more on TV than she did in real life. And that wasn't working out.

Without even thinking, Fiona bit into the corned beef sandwich that Mrs. Miltenberger packed. She even chewed and swallowed it.

The next thing she knew, her best friend was waving her hand in front of Fiona's face. "Hello?" said Cleo Button.

"Huh?" Fiona's brain snapped back to Ordinary. She swallowed. Why did she have that awful taste in her mouth?

"What's the matter?" said Cleo.

Fiona pulled apart her sandwich and examined its insides. "Ugh. Corned beef." She gulped her milk to wash away the taste.

Cleo cracked her knuckles. "Maybe your mom will come here."

Milo and Harold shot Cleo a Doom Scowl loaded with extra Doom, because Fiona's mom living in California had been a sore subject lately. Which apparently Cleo had forgotten.

"Sorry," Cleo whispered.

Fiona passed her sandwich to Harold. "Maybe I'll just go to California myself."

Harold and Milo laughed. Cleo said, "Good one."

Fiona felt her cheeks burn. "What's so funny? I could go to California. I could."

"Sure," said Milo.

"I mean it," said Fiona. "I could."

Harold bit into Fiona's sandwich and said, "Grandma says you can do anything that you set your mind to."

Fiona nodded and smiled. "See?" And then she covered Harold's mouth with her hand. "That's gross, Harold."

Harold swallowed and pushed her hand away. "But there's no way she would approve of you going to California all by your lonesome."

Fiona huffed. "Fine."

Milo jumped in. "You haven't ever been on ̨ airplane before, have you?"

"What does that have to do with anything?" said Fiona.

"It has to do with the fact that kids aren't allowed to get on airplanes by themselves if they've never been on one before," said Milo. "It's a rule."

"I never heard of that rule," said Cleo.

"You're making that up," said Fiona.

"Am not," he said. "My brother told me about it. And he's in eleventh grade, so he knows."

"Fiona has too been on a plane before," said Harold. "Remember when we went to the airplane museum last year and we got to sit inside the cockpit?"

"You're not helping, Harold," said Fiona.

Chapter 2

Not on your life," said Dad when he handed her a bowl of Sugar-Os. "You're only nine years old and you want me to let you get on an airplane all by yourself and fly all the way across the country, ALL BY YOURSELF?"

"I'm nine," said Fiona. "Not *only* nine. And that's old enough to do lots of things."

"And I'm six!" announced Max, beside her. He shifted his swim goggles over his eyes, stuck his face into his cereal, and tried to scoop up his Os with his tongue.

One look at that and Fiona declared, "I don't want Sugar-Os." She handed the bowl right back to Dad.

"I'll take them," said Max. He lifted his face from the bowl, and milk dripped from his goggles.

Fiona stared at an orange Sugar-O clinging to his cheek. "I want to eat a more grown-up breakfast."

Dad slid his cereal bowl across the table to her and said, "Okay. But you're not going to like it."

The flakes in Dad's bowl looked like tree bark. "It's brown." In her experience, brown food was almost always bad.

"It's bran," said Dad.

Even the name sounded brown. She picked up one flake and turned it over. She sniffed it and then touched it against her tongue.

Dad shook his head. "Why don't you just stick with yours?"

"No thanks," Fiona said, dropping the flake and raising a spoonful of brown to her mouth. "This is what grown-ups eat, this is what I'm going to eat from now on."

At first Fiona didn't think it was going to be so bad. But the chewing went on for a lot longer than she expected. Fiona began to wonder if trying to act like a grown-up might be too gross for her to take.

The chewing soon got to be too much. When she couldn't handle it any longer, she spit it all back into the bowl.

"Fiona!" said Dad.

"Whoa, cool," said Max, and he spit out his cereal into his bowl.

Dad gripped the table. "Max!"

Fiona wiped her tongue with her napkin and coughed. "Needs some sugar is all. Now, about California."

"The answer is no, young lady," said Dad.

"Can *I* go to California?" said Max.

Fiona and Dad said "no" at the same time.

"Why not?" said Max.

Fiona sighed. "Maybe when you're older," she said. "Right, Dad?"

Dad nodded and took a bite of his cereal. "And when you get a job and can pay for your own ticket."

"How much does a ticket cost?" said Fiona.

"A lot."

"I've got forty-eight dollars saved up," she said. She had been saving her allowance for the last year.

"I've got more money than you," said Max.

"Do not," said Fiona.

"Do too."

"How much can you have? You're only six, and I've been getting an allowance for longer than you."

"But you don't have your own business," Max said. "Like I do."

"What business?"

"Stickers," he said. "I make stickers. And sell them. Want to buy one?" He pulled out a sheet of yellow circles from his book bag. There were funny faces drawn on some of them and on others words like "Hi" and "Bye" and "I like TV." He held one out that said YOU ARE NICE.

Fiona smiled and reached for the sticker.

"That will be twenty-five cents," said Max.

Fiona rolled her eyes and shook her head. "No way."

"Fine," he said. Then he wrote something else on the sticker and handed it to her. "Here, you can have this one." Fiona read it: YOU ARE *NOT* NICE.

Later that day, Fiona dialed her mom's number. Her mom answered on the fifth ring. And right away, Fiona knew something was wrong.

"I'm having a day," said her mom. "The soap is in trouble."

"What kind of trouble?"

"Money trouble," she said. "The worst kind."

Fiona understood. "I'm having money trouble too. On account of the fact that I want to come out to California to see you, but I don't have enough money for an airplane ticket."

"Oh, that's sweet, Fiona honey. But I think we should all be saving our pennies. Besides, the last thing I need to worry about right now is my baby girl traveling across the country by herself."

"I'm not a baby," Fiona said.

"That's not what I meant, sweetie," said Mom. "I just meant that you're a little young to do something like that. Wait until you're older."

"I'll be older tomorrow."

"Fiona."

"But I will be!"

"You know I would love for you to come out here for a visit," said Mom. "One day you will."

An answer like that was a "no" in disguise. And if there was one thing that Fiona hated, it was an answer all dressed up like a *Y-E-S* but really when you got down to it was just a regular *N-O*. "When?" she pressed.

Mom said, "We'll see each other soon enough, baby."

But that wasn't soon enough. Not for Fiona.

• Chapter 3 •

Can I help you with that?" Fiona asked Mrs. Miltenberger, who was carrying folded laundry into Max's room.

Mrs. Miltenberger used her rump to open the door. "I've pretty much got it handled, thanks."

"But I want to." Fiona reached for the clothes but was only able to get hold of a pair of Max's tube socks before Mrs. Miltenberger lifted her arms and swung the load away.

"Fiona, please," she said. "I appreciate the thought, but it will go a lot faster if I—"

Fiona leapt at the pile of clothes and this time caught a handful. "I can help!" she said, sometime between the jump and the realization that the pile of folded clothes was headed for the floor.

"Fiona!" shouted Mrs. Miltenberger.

Fiona looked at the floor. It was amazing how quickly clothes could become unfolded. And unpiled. "Sorry. I didn't mean for that to happen."

Mrs. Miltenberger sat down on the edge of Max's bed and pointed to the laundry all over the floor. "What on earth is the matter with you?"

"I just wanted to help," said Fiona.

"And a nice job you did of it, I'd say." Mrs. Miltenberger shook her head and then bent over, stretching her arms toward the clothes. She let out a groan as she snatched up one of Max's T-shirts. Then she pointed to the rest of the mess. "If you're in such a helping mood, why don't you give me a hand?"

"All right." Fiona dove for the floor and scooped

up the clothes. She held them tight to her chest. When one started to come undone near the top, she clamped her neck on it. "Look," she said to Mrs. Miltenberger, careful not to lose her grip. "I've got them all."

"Except for the pair of underwear by your feet." Mrs. Miltenberger patted the spot on the bed beside her. "Put them here, please."

Fiona looked at her feet and saw Max's underwear. "Is that the only one?"

"The only one what?"

She turned her face away and felt the clothes shift in her arms. "The only pair of underwear."

Mrs. Miltenberger folded Max's T-shirt and laid it on the bed beside her. "Of course not. There's a week's worth in there. Hurry up and bring them here, please. You're about to drop everything."

But it was too late. Fiona *did* drop everything. "Ewwww!" she shouted, jumping up and down, while brushing off the gazillions of underwear germs that had infected her. "Gross!"

"For mercy's sake!" said Mrs. Miltenberger. "It's clean laundry. It's all been cleaned."

This made absolutely no difference to Fiona. Clean or not, she was not going to touch anything. NO SIRREE BOB. She surveyed the items on the floor. "How about if I just pick up the T-shirts and pants?"

"Fine," said Mrs. Miltenberger.

Fiona picked up Max's T-shirts and pants. "Do I have to fold them, too?"

Mrs. Miltenberger said, "Oh, blessed, just leave them!"

"Thanks," said Fiona. She looked around Max's room. "When I'm done helping you with this, what's next?"

"When you're done *helping* me?" said Mrs. Miltenberger. "That's what you said?"

"Yep," said Fiona.

"Huh." Mrs. Miltenberger raised her eyebrows. "Thought so. Just checking."

"So what are you going to do next?" said Fiona.

Mrs. Miltenberger took in a breath and then blew it out with enough force to make her lips sputter. "Dishes, I suppose."

"I'm on it," said Fiona.

"Don't even think about it," said Mrs. Miltenberger, holding up her hand.

"Well, there must be something else I can help with," said Fiona.

Mrs. Miltenberger stuffed the last of Max's clothes into a drawer and then headed downstairs. Fiona trailed behind. "More laundry?" Fiona asked, pointing to a basket of folded clothes by the couch.

"Always," said Mrs. Miltenberger.

"I can put it away," said Fiona as she got closer to the basket. Then she stopped, not too close, and eyed it from a safe distance. It looked like mostly her dad's clothes. "Wait. Is there more underwear in there?"

"Tell you what," said Mrs. Miltenberger as she pushed open the door to the kitchen. She picked up the metal watering can from on top of the refrigerator. "Here." She tossed the can to Fiona. "The plants are thirsty."

Fiona was not very good at catching things, so she got out of the way and let the watering can hit the end of the couch. It bounced underneath the coffee table.

"You could've had that one," said Mrs. Miltenberger.

"You threw it too hard," Fiona complained. She scooped up the can by the handle and followed Mrs. Miltenberger into the kitchen. As she filled the watering can at the sink, she practiced her pirouettes. "Are you sure there isn't something else I can do? Something bigger? I mean something that would show you how grown up and responsible I am?"

"Grown up and responsible?" said Mrs. Miltenberger.

"Yep."

"Huh. I thought that was what you said." Mrs. Miltenberger scratched her head. "Just checking."

Mrs. Miltenberger warned her to be careful, not to fill it too full, not to spill it on anything, and not to do something else that Fiona didn't really pay any attention to. "Don't worry," said Fiona, shutting off the faucet. "I think I can water some plants."

"Famous last words," said Mrs. Miltenberger.

Fiona didn't know what that meant. But she was about to be the best waterer that Mrs. Miltenberger ever laid eyes on. She visited the plants on the shelf in the living room first, a fern and a spider plant whose thin green and white leaves hung low. She carefully tilted the watering can over each one and let them have a drink. "Easy peasy," said Fiona.

She hauled the watering can over to the lemon
tree on a stand by the front window. Her dad had
always said it was a lemon tree, but Fiona never
saw lemons on it, not even one. It was a lemon
of a lemon tree if you asked her. She emptied the
watering can into the pot and watched the water
disappear into the dirt. "Still thirsty?"

Back into the kitchen she went for a refill. Mrs. Miltenberger, who was busy putting away dishes, said, "How's it going?"

"Fine and dandy," Fiona replied, seeing how many pirouettes she could fit in before the water reached the top of the can. She spun around counting twelve and then yanked the watering can from the sink, splashing only a tiny bit on the counter.

"Careful," Mrs. Miltenberger said.

Fiona was back at the lemon tree in no time at all, and in one turn of her wrist she emptied the watering can again. "Maybe now we'll get some lemons," she told the tree. Fiona swung the can around as she practiced more pirouettes, to celebrate the fruit that would surely come from such good and responsible watering. But on the fifth pirouette, her feet got all wobbly and knocked the can against the terra-cotta pot. The can fell to the floor, and she quickly put her hands on the pot to steady it. Knocking over a lemon tree, even a lemon of a lemon tree, would not be a very grown-up thing to do.

She picked up the watering can to return it to the kitchen. And that's when she saw water running out of the pot. At first it was only a little bit. Her dad, who was a meteorologist, would have called it a "light drizzle." It trickled from the side of the pot, where Fiona now saw there was a crack, and then onto the wooden plant stand. She put her hand on top of the crack to keep the water in, and that's when the gushing started. A downpour, really.

Fiona thought fast. She looked around the room and grabbed some clothes from the laundry basket next to the couch. She sopped up the water from the carpet with a couple of her dad's work shirts and then went back for more. She grabbed a hand-ful of clothes, and for a second, she wondered if there was any underwear in there. She hoped there wasn't, but in an emergency, there was no time to check for underwear. And this was an emergency.

Fiona strung some of the clothes around the bottom of the pot to catch the water before it reached the carpet. And then she stuffed the rest of the clothes right into the dirt to soak up what hadn't yet made it out. That seemed to do the trick. Except for a few drips, the rain had stopped. Fiona stood back and admired her quick thinking.

The admiration didn't last very long, though, because right about that time Mrs. Miltenberger finished doing the dishes. "Blazes!" she shouted, covering her eyes with her hands. "What have you done?"

Fiona started to explain, but Mrs. Miltenberger cut her off and yelled, "Out! Out! Out!" She pointed to the door with a look on her face that was usually reserved for Max.

This was some kind of thanks she got for trying to help. Fiona trudged over to the door, feeling as un—grown up as ever.

• Chapter 4 •

Fiona trudged down Juniper Street. She didn't know where she was going. But that was the thing about trudging—you just kept going and going and didn't know where you'd end up.

She trudged across Ordinary. The whole time she wondered why you couldn't just say you were grown up and then actually *be* grown up. Why did it have to be so hard? Always, so hard. And when would it happen? Would she just wake up one day and then somebody would say, "Good morning,

Fiona Finkelstein, you are now officially a grown-up and you can do anything you want, including getting a monkey!"?

Fiona wondered what it felt like to be a grown-up. She figured at the very least it must feel like you've got bags of sand tied to your toes because every grown-up she knew was on the slow side and seemed tired an awful lot. Just in case, she checked her feet at every corner. But they didn't feel any heavier. And she couldn't feel any sand, no grit between her toes.

Fiona was continuing her trudge along the north side of Baker's Park when she saw something that made her feet stop dead. On the other side of the park, across the Great Lawn and next to the clock tower, she saw a boy holding a leash. And on the other end of that leash was a chicken.

She had seen people walk all sorts of things before—dogs, cats, ferrets, rabbits even. At the mall, sometimes she even saw little kids on leashes. Which Mrs. Miltenberger always said was a "disgrace" and that you'd never catch her putting Max on a leash no matter how much of a darter he was. And no matter how much Fiona said she should.

But never before had Fiona seen a boy walking a chicken.

She watched for a while, watched as they walked along like it was the most perfectly ordinary thing to do. Some people came up to them, others pointed, but this boy and this chicken did not stop for anyone. They crossed the street, and she lost sight of them for a moment behind a line of parked cars. When they made a left turn down Washington Avenue, Fiona was afraid that she'd lose sight of them for good. So she started to run.

It surprised her how quickly she made it across the Great Lawn. She turned left on Washington Avenue, just like they did, expecting them to be right there. But except for a man pulling weeds out of the cracks in the sidewalk, the street was empty.

"Did you see a boy with a chicken?" Fiona shouted to the guy pulling weeds. She bent over and rested her hands on her knees to catch her breath.

"With a what?"

"A chicken," she said. "He was walking a chicken!"

The man shook his head and muttered, "Crazy girl. Why would a person walk a chicken?"

This was exactly what Fiona wanted to know. She ran to the end of the street, checking the sidewalk for clues like feathers or chicken scratch or eggs. Nothing. She circled back toward the park and wandered up and down the side streets asking anybody she met if they had seen the chicken boy. No one had.

After a while, with no sign of either the boy or the chicken, she began to wonder if she really had seen what she thought she saw. Or if all that trudging made her see things that weren't there. Maybe, she thought, the chicken boy was mysterious like Bigfoot, out there somewhere but hardly ever seen.

As she headed back home, Fiona thought about how searching for Bigfoot must be a very hard job, one that was probably meant for grown-ups, on account of the fact that Bigfoot is probably big all over (not just his foot) and only a grown-up would be brave enough to face him. And also because it was common knowledge that Bigfoot ate kids like candy.

Bigfoot hunter was not the kind of job Fiona would ever want; that she knew for sure. Still, if you wanted to prove that you were grown up and responsible, catching Bigfoot would be a surefire way to do it, Fiona thought. Actually, you'd probably have to be pretty grown up on the inside to have any kind of job at all.

She sat on the curb to rest her tired legs. She looked around. In her search for the chicken boy, Fiona hadn't paid too close attention to where she'd ended up. So many of these streets looked the same—houses, trees, porch swings. Same, same. But as soon as she saw the red brick building on the corner, Fiona knew exactly where she was. And she had an idea!

She made her tired legs run again, across the street

and up the stairs to La Petite Academy. The door to the practice room was closed, but Fiona watched through the glass panel. Madame Vallee stood at the front of the class with the heels of her fancy black shoes pressed tightly together. She nodded as the girls practiced the *rond de jambe* at the bar.

Fiona went into the hall and waited for the class to end. While she waited, she watched a tiny spider crawl up the pink wall and disappear behind a picture frame. Fiona wondered if the spider was just out for a stroll or if it had made a home behind the frame. Or if it was simply paying someone a visit, on account of the fact that its father and everybody else in Spiderland thought it was grown up enough to do things by itself.

Finally the door swung open and all of the girls flooded the hall with high-pitched chatter on their way to the dressing room. Fiona pressed herself against the wall to get out of their way, and when they passed, she slipped into the practice room.

"The early bird eats the worm, Fiona?" Madame Vallee said. "You are two days early for lesson."

Fiona followed her to the CD player on a table against the back wall. "I wanted to ask you a question."

Madame Vallee removed a CD from the player and slid it into a plastic sleeve. "What is it, my darling?"

"I've been noticing lately that you look really tired." This was not true, of course. Madame Vallee always looked very nice and very awake, but this was the only way Fiona thought she might be able to get what she wanted.

Madame Vallee smoothed her hair with her fingers and adjusted a pin in her bun. "How is this a question? Tired? What do you say to me? This is a joke, yes?"

Fiona shook her head. "I'm just saying that you must be working too hard."

Madame Vallee raised her eyebrows. "Yes, well, the hard work does not do itself."

"You're not a spring chicken, you know," said Fiona. "You need to get some rest. I saw on TV the other day that women your age are on the go too much and don't get enough rest."

Madame Vallee put both hands on the bar and leaned against it. "My gracious. Well, tell me. What did TV say I should do?"

"It said you should ask for help," said Fiona.

"It said I should ask for some help?" asked Madame Vallee.

"Well, not you exactly, but, you know, women your age and stuff." Fiona cleared her throat. "I mean, I think you could use some help around here."

Madame Vallee looked at the ceiling and seemed to give this some thought. "What would I get help with?"

"You know, with the ballet teaching and things like that."

"I have had thought about part-time teacher," she said. "My classes are quite large in size."

"See?" Fiona clapped.

"Thank you, Fiona," said Madame Vallee. She cupped Fiona's chin with her palm. "You are a very sweet girl, as well as a good dancer. I will consider it."

"When do I start? I mean, after you are done considering it."

"Start?" said Madam Vallee.

"Being your helper."

"Oh, you didn't think . . ." Madame Vallee gently brushed Fiona's cheek and laughed. "No, no, my darling. You cannot possibly be helper."

"Why not? You said . . ."

"I was thinking of my niece," she said. "She is older. But don't worry, not old like me. She still is spring chicken."

"But I can do lots of things to help you," said Fiona. "I've been taking ballet lessons from you for a long time, so I know what stuff needs to be done around here."

"That is very true." Madame Vallee rested her hand on Fiona's arm. "Thank you for your offer. If you were a tiny bit older, I would snap you up like this." She raised both hands above her head and clicked her fingers.

"But you should snap me up like that now," said Fiona, clicking her fingers at Madame Vallee in return, "because I'll be a tiny bit older really soon. Like now. I'm older now than I was a few seconds ago. And now. I'm older again. And again!"

Madame Vallee laughed. She rested her hand on her chest, and her fingers danced at her neck. "You're a comedienne."

"A what?" asked Fiona.

"You make me laugh always." Madame Vallee glided across the practice room and out the door.

That was good and all, but it didn't help Fiona much. Really not at all.

• Chapter 5 •

The next day at school, before the first bell, Fiona told Cleo how she gave Madame Vallee the idea to hire a helper. And then how Madame gave the job to somebody else. "What other kinds of jobs are there?"

Cleo shook her head. "Don't know."

"Hey," said Fiona. "You have a job. Maybe I could get a job at your mom and dad's restaurant."

Cleo raised her eyebrows. "Doing what?"

"I don't know. The things that you do, like filling salt and pepper shakers and ketchup bottles.

Saying hello to people and taking them to their table."

"You want a job saying hello to people?" said Cleo.

"Not just hello," said Fiona. "I also said I'd take them to their table."

"That's *my* job," said Cleo. "And so is wrapping silverware, filling salt and pepper shakers."

"And ketchup?"

"That too."

"Well, what else is there to do?"

Cleo shrugged. "Cook, deliver food, run the cash register."

"Ooh, the cash register," said Fiona. "I'll do that."

"No, you won't," said Cleo, cracking her knuckles. "My mom does. And you have to be at least sixteen to cook or wait tables. Maybe you could scrape the food off the plates before they go into the dishwasher."

Fiona groaned. "Would I have to touch the food?"

"It usually just slides off into the trash can," said Cleo.

"What if the food doesn't want to come off the plate? Then would I have to touch it?"

Cleo sighed. "You'd have gloves on."

"So I'd have to touch the food with gloves on?"

Cleo's face got red. But before she could say anything, Mr. Bland handed a stack of papers to Cleo and asked her to hand them out. Fiona panicked. Mr. Bland liked to give a quiz when you were least expecting it, which was one of a very long list of reasons why Mr. Bland was Fiona's least favorite teacher in the whole entire world.

When Fiona got her paper, she was relieved to find that it wasn't a quiz. It was a map of the Great Ordinary Fair. Every building, pavilion, and snack shop was marked, and at the center of it all was the Great Ferris Wheel—a giant *O* for "Ordinary." When it was lit up, you could see it from miles away. Looping through all of the buildings and rides were paths that on the map looked like strings of spaghetti. And handwritten on each path were *X*s and the names of the kids in Fiona's class.

"I've divided up our class into groups of two," Mr. Bland explained. "And you'll find your names next to an *X* on this map. This is where you'll be stationed."

Fiona found her name along with Cleo's next to Bridgette's Mum Stand, where they sold chrysanthemums in big plastic pots. Nobody ever went to Bridgette's Mum Stand. It was the farthest *X* from the rides and farm animals. Fiona didn't have anything against mums—they were a perfectly fine and dandy flower—but nobody came to the Great Ordinary Fair to buy a flowerpot that they'd have to lug around the whole time.

Which meant that nobody would be in Fiona and Cleo's area, which meant that Fiona and Cleo would have nobody to give maps to.

"Not fair!" was what Fiona was thinking. And

then what she was thinking accidentally came out of her mouth.

"Excuse me?" said Mr. Bland.

Fiona held up the map and pointed to the X with her name on it. "But we're way far away from all the fun stuff. You know, where all the people will be. Who are we supposed to give maps to over there?"

Mr. Bland said, "If you'd like to skip the fair altogether, that can be arranged. Just keep talking."

Cleo looked at Fiona and mouthed, *Stop.* Which is what Fiona did. Right after she said, "But can't we at least be near the Ferris wheel or something?"

Cleo put her head down on her desk as Mr. Bland said, "Why don't you take a walk down the hall to Principal Sterling's office. Milo, please make sure she doesn't get lost."

"I know how to get there," Fiona told Milo once they were in the hall.

"Why did you keep talking after he warned you?" said Milo. "What did you think was going to happen?"

Fiona shrugged. "Sometimes words just come out of my mouth before I know what's happening. And then it's too late."

Milo shook his head. "I know."

They reached Principal Sterling's office, and Milo left Fiona with Mrs. Little, the school secretary. She was busy typing at her computer and didn't see Fiona standing there at first. But when she finally looked away from her screen, she sighed and said, "What is it this time, Fiona?"

"Mr. Bland sent me down here to talk to Principal Sterling."

"About?"

"Complaining too much, I think."

"You think?" said Mrs. Little.

Fiona nodded.

"Hold on a minute." Mrs. Little knocked on Principal Sterling's door and then stuck her head inside. Fiona heard her name and some whispering, but she couldn't make out the words. Mrs. Little returned to her desk and said, "Go on in, Fiona."

Fiona crossed the room and slowly pushed open the door to Principal Sterling's office. Principal Sterling closed a folder on her desk and waved Fiona in. "Have a seat," she said. "You and Mr. Bland are having another difficult day?"

Fiona nodded and tried to explain. But Principal Sterling held her hand up in the air until Fiona got quiet. Then she took off her red glasses, which Fiona had always liked, rubbed her eyes, and said, "Mr. Bland is your teacher, and you need to remember your place in his classroom, Fiona."

"But . . ."

Principal Sterling held up her hand again. "You're in fourth grade, and you should know how to listen and follow rules by now. It's Mr. Bland's job to make sure you learn what you need to learn. But you have a job, too. Your job is to listen and follow the rules so that you *can* learn."

Fiona thought that scraping food (with gloves on) sounded like a better job than listening and following Mr. Bland's rules. Especially when the rules weren't fair. Besides, what was she supposed to learn by handing out maps to nobody? Nothing, if you asked her.

Principal Sterling put her elbows on her desk

and leaned forward. "So, let's cooperate and try to act a little bit more grown up."

"But I am trying," said Fiona. Why couldn't anybody see that?

• Chapter 6 •

After school, Fiona climbed into the Bingo Bus and said hello to Mrs. Miltenberger and the Broads in the backseat. "Fiona Finkelstein, how's it going, lovey?" said Mrs. O'Brien.

Fiona had gotten used to telling the Bingo Broads some of her troubles in the past. They were always very eager to give advice. Sometimes too eager. And not all of their advice was bad, but after a couple of rotten apples, Fiona had decided it was better for everyone if she didn't follow what they said.

"Fine and dandy," said Fiona. Then she noticed the blue boot on Mrs. Lordeau's foot. "What happened?"

"Oh, the dumbest thing," she said. "I was hunting for spices in my cupboard and fell off a footstool. It's just a sprain, but I'm supposed to stay off it."

"Does it hurt?" asked Fiona.

Mrs. Lordeau patted the top of the boot. "Not enough to keep me from bingo. But it's going to hurt Mayflower more than it hurts me."

"You and that dog," said Mrs. Huff.

"Poor boy, I won't be able to take him on his walks like this," said Mrs. Lordeau. "At least not for a couple of weeks."

"Enough about you," said Mrs. O'Brien. "I want to hear about Fiona. Violet here tells us that you are quite the helper at home, sugar."

Mrs. Miltenberger pulled away from the curb and eyed Fiona in the rearview mirror.

"You told?" Fiona felt her cheeks burn.

Mrs. Miltenberger grinned and shrugged. "I might have said something about it. All in good fun."

Fiona stuck her hand in the air to protest. "In my defense, nobody told me that Max's underwear would be involved. And that crack in the lemon tree pot could have been there all along. You don't know."

The Broads laughed. "I don't blame you at all, Fiona," said Mrs. Huff. "Laundry is the worst."

Mrs. O'Brien ran her fingers through her short hair. "What's the root cause of this sudden need to help?"

"I want a job," said Fiona plainly.

"A job," said Mrs. Lordeau. "Now what kind of job are you looking for, honey?"

"You're too young for a job," said Mrs. O'Brien. "You've got the rest of your life to work, so you should be enjoying your time now."

"Nothing wrong with a little hard work, if you

ask me," said Mrs. Huff. "I started helping my father wash windows when I was just eight years old. Hard work puts hair on your chest."

"The girl doesn't need hair on her chest, Gert," said Mrs. O'Brien.

Mrs. Miltenberger said, "Fiona does work. She gives weather reports at WORD. She's the ballerina weathergirl."

"Well," said Fiona, "I don't do that as much anymore."

Mrs. Huff played with the mole on her chin. "Fiona, now you listen to me. Your job is to do well in your subjects at school. That's enough. Don't grow up too fast, hear."

"That's right, Fiona. You be like that Peter Pan," said Mrs. O'Brien.

"Don't tell her that, Fanny," said Mrs. Lordeau. "Fiona doesn't want to be like Peter Pan. The girl has to grow up sometime."

Mrs. O'Brien smacked the seat with her hand.

"Now just what is wrong with Peter Pan?"

A lot of the time, the things that grown-ups said were confusing. Principal Sterling wanted Fiona to act grown up, and so did Mr. Bland. And so did Fiona, for that matter. Being grown up meant being able to do more stuff. "Don't you like being a grown-up?" Fiona asked.

"It's not that," said Mrs. Huff. "It's just that it's so much more fun to be your age."

Fiona nodded just to be polite. They were old and must have forgotten what it was like to be nine going on ten and not be allowed to do anything. Fiona stared out the window while the Broads argued about whether it would be better to be able to fly or never get old.

Fiona shook her head. It was an easy choice. She'd rather be able to fly. Because then she wouldn't need permission to get on an airplane to go to California and see her mom. She could just go anytime she wanted. She imagined herself lifting off, right then, right through the roof of the Bingo Bus. She was about to soar when she saw bright red balloons out the window. "What's that?" She followed the red balloons to a sign that read GRAND OPENING and to another one that read THE FISH HUT.

"Stop the bus!" shouted Fiona.

"Glory days!" said Mrs. Miltenberger, hitting the brakes.

"Peter, Paul, and Mary!" said Mrs. O'Brien.

"Gracious!" said Mrs. Huff.

Mrs. Lordeau clutched her chest and gasped. "I've already got one leg in a boot! Are you trying to finish me off?"

"What on earth is the matter, Fiona?" said Mrs. Miltenberger, turning around in her seat.

Fiona pointed out the window. "Can we go in there?"

Mrs. Miltenberger gave Fiona a Doom Scowl with Two Helpings of Maximum Doom. "Have you lost your mind hollering like that?"

"Sorry. Can we?" Fiona kept her eyes on the store.

"I don't think so," said Mrs. Miltenberger, turning back around.

"Come on, Violet," said Mrs. O'Brien. "Let's go in. I've been wanting a goldfish. You know, for some company."

"Company?" said Mrs. Miltenberger.

"Everybody needs some company."

"Just pull in there," said Mrs. Lordeau, pointing to an open parking space. "We're all going in."

Fiona smiled at the Bingo Broads. Mrs. Miltenberger shook her head, but it was four against one. Mrs. Miltenberger found a parking space in the lot across the street, and when she turned off the bus, Fiona was the first one out.

She didn't wait for the others before darting inside. The Fish Hut was filled with shelves, three rows high, of bubbling fish tanks. Each tank was filled with colorful fish, some so electric they could have been plugged in.

"What kind of fish are you interested in, Fiona?" asked Mrs. Lordeau, as she hobbled inside on her crutches.

"Oh, I don't want a fish," said Fiona.

"You don't? Then why . . ."

"May I help you?" said a man holding a green net. His shirt pocket had the name Rick sewed on it with dark blue thread.

"You can help me," Fiona said. "I'd like to work here."

He laughed and patted Fiona on the shoulder. Then he asked Mrs. Lordeau, "Are you interested in a fish? For our grand opening, all of our goldfish are on sale. Twenty percent off."

"Oh, I'm not really a fish person," said Mrs. Lordeau, eyeing the bubbling tanks. "Dogs are more my speed. But my friend here is looking for employment. Perhaps you have something she could do?"

Rick smiled at Mrs. Lordeau and then looked

Fiona over. She was glad she had worn matching socks today. "I'm not hiring. But if you'd like to look at some fish . . ."

"I can do lots of things," said Fiona. She walked over to a fish tank that had a thick, gray fish with long whiskers resting on the bottom. She knocked on the glass real hard until the fish swam to the back of the tank behind a rock. Then she turned to Rick and said, "See? I'm a good fish rouser. Which would come in handy because the last thing people want to buy is a sleepy fish."

Rick's hand clutched his shirt. Then he pointed to a sign hanging above the top row of fish tanks. "Little girl, what does that say?"

Fiona read the sign out loud. "Please do not tap on the glass." Then she understood. "Oh, sorry about that. But then how do you wake up the fish?"

"Wake up the . . . ?" Rick scratched his head and then turned his attention to Mrs. Miltenberger and the rest of the Bingo Broads, who were examining some striped fish. "Good afternoon. How may I help you?" He eyeballed Fiona a couple of times until Fiona shoved her hands into her pockets to show him that she was going to let sleeping fish alone.

Mrs. O'Brien said, "I'm interested in a low-maintenance type of fish. Preferably one that isn't too temperamental."

"She doesn't want a fish who thinks she's a diva," said Mrs. Miltenberger.

"That's right. My life only has room for one diva, and that's me."

Rick said, "I'm sure we can find a fish suited to your needs." He led Mrs. O'Brien to the fish tanks near Fiona.

"What about this one?" Fiona pointed to the fish she woke up, careful to keep her finger off the glass. "There. Behind that rock."

Mrs. O'Brien brought her face close to the glass

and peered into the tank. "An uglier face I have not seen," she said.

Rick cleared his throat. "That's a catfish. A scavenger. It will eat almost anything and helps keep the aquarium clean."

"I do like a fish that cleans up after itself," she said.

"And it likes to take a lot of naps," said Fiona. "Not catnaps, but cat*fish* naps."

Mrs. O'Brien and Mrs. Miltenberger laughed

at Fiona's joke, but Rick brought his lips together in such a way that Fiona guessed he didn't have a sense of humor when it came to fish.

Fiona pointed to another catfish in the next tank. It was pressed up against the side of the tank so you could see its underneath side. "This one is trying to get out!"

Rick said, "He's eating the algae off the glass."

"That's the one you should get, Mrs. O'Brien," said Fiona. "It even does windows!"

"Sold." Mrs. O'Brien tapped on the glass and said to her new fish, "Pack your bags, because you are coming home with me." Then she turned toward Fiona and pinched her cheek. "You, my lovey, have a future in sales."

Fiona smiled at Rick then, as if to say, "What do you have to say about that job now?"

But he just shook his head at Fiona and asked Mrs. O'Brien, "What size is your aquarium at home?"

"I don't have an aquarium," she said.

"No matter." He scooped Mrs. O'Brien's fish into a plastic bag full of water. "We have everything you need here."

Fiona watched him wind the top of the bag around his fingers and then thread it into a knot. "How about a fish for you?" he said.

"Me?" said Fiona. "I don't know. I want to get a monkey, but my dad keeps saying no."

Rick held up the bag and looked Mrs. O'Brien's fish in the eye. "A lot of responsibility, taking care of a pet. Maybe you're not ready."

Fiona felt her cheeks get hot. Then she reached into her pocket and pulled out a few crinkled dollars and some change. She quickly scanned the fish tanks. She'd rather have a monkey. That she knew for sure, because how much fun could a tiny fish be, anyway? Then a yellow sign in the shape of a sunburst caught her eye. The sign was taped to a corner of a small fish tank behind the register. "What are those?" she said, pointing.

"Pollywogs," said Rick.

"Pollywogs?" said Fiona. "Are they as fun as their name sounds?"

"Pollywogs," he repeated. "You know, tadpoles." He cleared his throat and opened his eyes wide. "Frogs."

Fiona didn't know much more about frogs than she knew about fish. But there was one thing she did know: frogs have legs. And by her account, that made them closer to monkeys than fish. She looked for Mrs. Miltenberger to make sure it was okay, but she was all the way at the other end of the store with Mrs. O'Brien. So Fiona handed her crumpled money over to Rick. "Sold!"

Chapter 7

Fiona stared at her pollywog the whole ride home. "I'm not seeing any legs yet."

"Next time you get an idea to bring home a critter, I wish you'd ask me first," said Mrs. Miltenberger. "Your father may not be too pleased."

"I'll take good care of him," Fiona said. "Mr. Funbucket won't get into any trouble."

"It's not him I'm worried about."

"When will he get some legs?" Fiona asked.

"Rick said it could take a couple of months," said Mrs. O'Brien. "Have patience."

"But Mr. Funbucket looks like he's ready to start walking," said Fiona. "Hey! He just looked right at me when I said his name." She pressed her face against the bag. "Mr. Funbucket. Mr. Funbucket. Mr. Funbucket. There! He did it again!" She held the bag out for Mrs. Miltenberger to see.

"Not while I'm driving!" she said, pushing the bag away.

Fiona continued to stare. "Still no legs."

. . .

. . .

"Still none."

"Fiona," said Mrs. Miltenberger. "Please."

"Nope. Still none."

"Where did you get that?" said Max when he came home from swim practice.

"The Fish Hut."

"What's that?" he asked, sliding his swim goggles to the top of his head.

"Just a place." Being a pet owner made Fiona feel very grown up. So grown up that she didn't feel the need to share every detail about her day with Max. And also because she didn't want him to think he was grown up enough to have a pollywog or any other kind of pet that had legs (or would have them sometime soon).

"Where's Mrs. M.?" said Max.

"Next door, getting something for me."

"What is she getting?"

Fiona set the bag with Mr. Funbucket in it on the coffee table. Then she folded her arms across her chest. "Max, it's grown-up stuff. You wouldn't understand."

Max stuck his nose in the air and in a high-pitched voice that sounded something like Fiona's said, "It's grown-up stuff. Oooooh. And you just wouldn't understand." Then he stuck out his tongue and stomped off to his room.

Mrs. Miltenberger opened the front door and held up a fishbowl. "I found it! I knew I had one from when Mr. Miltenberger, rest his soul, got me a pair of hermit crabs years ago on a trip to Myrtle Beach. I never really took to them, the hermit crabs. Those legs, creepy." She handed the bowl to Fiona. "Anyway, they only lived for about a year or so, and I kept that bowl because you never know when a new critter is going to crawl back into your life. Or in your case, swim."

Fiona thanked Mrs. Miltenberger and then untied the knot at the top of the bag. She held the bag over the fish bowl and carefully poured in the water. Mr. Funbucket tried to stay in the bottom of the bag as long as he could, scared little fellow, but he finally gave up and slid into the bowl with a splash. "Welcome home," said Fiona. Mr. Funbucket flipped his tail and began to swim, which

Fiona translated to, *Thank you ever so kindly; my new home is just fine and dandy.* "I'll need to get you branches and rocks so you can climb once you sprout your legs," Fiona told him.

Fiona kept watch for any leg-sprouting activity until Dad came home from the news station. She thought she saw a leg spring forth at one point, but it turns out that pollywogs can go to the bathroom while they're swimming. "What's new, Bean?" Dad said, taking off his coat.

"This!" said Fiona, pointing to Mr. Funbucket. "He's a pollywog."

"I see that."

"He won't be for long, though, because he's going to get some legs soon and turn into a frog."

"That's what happens," he said, sighing. But legs must not have been as exciting to Dad as they were for Fiona, because he barely looked at Mr. Funbucket before he started going through the mail.

Fiona whispered to Mr. Funbucket, "That's my

dad. Usually he's pretty friendly, but sometimes he gets a little stressed at work. As long as you keep your room clean, you should get along with him fine."

On her way out the door, Mrs. Miltenberger tripped over one of Max's action figures that he left lying about on the floor. "Cursed things!" she yelled.

"Where's Max?" Dad said.

"In his room," answered Fiona, keeping her eyes on her pollywog.

"Go get him, please."

"MAX, GET DOWN HERE!" yelled Fiona as loud as she could.

Dad shook his head. "I asked you to go upstairs to get him, Fiona."

"Really, Fiona," said Mrs. Miltenberger.

"But I didn't want to miss Mr. Funbucket getting his legs," she said. "What kind of a responsible pet owner would I be if I missed that?"

Dad sighed and rubbed his forehead. Max's feet pounded the upstairs hallway. "Like a herd of elephants," said Mrs. Miltenberger.

"He's got his flippers on again," said Fiona. Max could make a lot of noise when he went places, but when he had his flippers on his feet, the walls shook.

"Careful on the stairs," hollered Mrs. Miltenberger. But she was too late, because as Fiona took her eyes off Mr. Funbucket for one second and glanced at the stairs, Max's left flipper folded under itself and sent Max down the last few steps in a tumble.

"What did I tell you about wearing those things in the house?" said Dad.

Max pulled himself up, straightened the towel he had draped over his shoulders as a cape, and gathered the bundle of swim medals he wore around his neck. "I'm okay," he said. "It takes more than a faulty flipper to keep Captain Seahorse down."

"Have a seat, Captain," said Dad. "I've got some news."

Fiona didn't like the way that sounded. Dad took a deep breath, and one side of his mouth curved up into a smile while the other side stayed where it was like it didn't know what to do. "What's the matter?" asked Fiona. Already her stomach churned. She crossed her fingers and made a wish that it wasn't cancer or divorce or getting braces. Lately, these were the three things that she worried about most.

It didn't help that Mrs. Miltenberger had a panicked look on her face. She said, "Should I stick around, Norm?"

Dad nodded. "You're family, Violet. Have a seat."

Fiona put her hand on Mr. Funbucket's bowl to let him know that it would be okay. Even though she wasn't so sure herself that it would be.

"Your mom called," he said.

Fiona put her arm over her stomach and held her breath.

"*Heartaches and Diamonds* is being canceled," said Dad. "Your mom is losing her job."

Fiona started breathing again. This was a lot less bad than cancer and divorce, at least. Her mom would find another job. And even if she didn't, she could come home, maybe. So then why did Dad and Mrs. Miltenberger look like their mouths were full of gravel?

"Bummer," said Max. He took off back upstairs. Nothing seemed to put a wrinkle in Captain Seahorse's cape. In Max's world, his biggest worry was whether he would get to watch cartoons after dinner or not.

Dad put his hand on Fiona's knee. "Now, I know how you worry, Fiona. And I don't want you to worry about this. We'll make it work. We may need to cut back on a few things, that's all. Until your mom finds a new job. Okay?"

Fiona nodded. She didn't know a lot about these kinds of things, but she did know that there was

almost always something to worry about. Especially when a grown-up told you there wasn't.
From upstairs, she heard Max shout, "Captain
Seahorse will save you!" And then he burst out
laughing. For a second, Fiona remembered what
it was like to live in that world, and for a second,
she missed it.

She swallowed hard. How did the gravel get in
her mouth?

• Chapter 8 •

During dinner, nobody talked about Mom losing her job. But Fiona could tell that it was on her dad's mind. And it was definitely on *her* mind. She tried to bury the worry, like she buried the asparagus under her mash potatoes, but even though she couldn't see it, she still knew it was there.

Mrs. Miltenberger put some of the leftovers into a plastic container. "I'm taking some food over to Mrs. Lordeau's. She's not a very good cook when both of her legs are working right, so I don't want to even imagine what a bad leg has done to her paltry skills. Anyone want to come?"

"Nope," said Max.

Fiona didn't feel much like doing anything, but Mrs. Miltenberger insisted. "It will do you some good, and don't worry, I guarantee you that Mr. Funbucket will not sprout legs in the time that we're gone."

Mrs. Lordeau only lived a few blocks away, but Mrs. Miltenberger didn't want to walk. "Cars are for driving," she said.

Fiona rang the doorbell. They waited for a gazillion years. Fiona rang the doorbell again. "Maybe she's not home."

"She's home," said Mrs. Miltenberger. "With that leg, she can't go anywhere. Keep ringing."

Fiona pressed the doorbell over and over again until she heard, "Hold your horses, I said I'm coming! And if you don't lay off that bell, you're going to get a close-up look at my crutch!"

Mrs. Miltenberger snickered and gently pulled Fiona's finger away from the bell.

There were a few whacks and thumps from inside before Mrs. Lordeau appeared at the door, leaning on her crutches. "I'm all right," said Mrs. Lordeau. "I don't know who put this furniture so close together."

"We brought you food," said Fiona, holding up a plastic container.

"You shouldn't have," she said. "But I'm so glad you did. Come in. Come in."

Fiona and Mrs. Miltenberger followed Mrs. Lordeau inside. Mrs. Miltenberger said, "Fiona, why don't you go ahead and put the food in the kitchen awhile."

Mrs. Lordeau's house was small, like a cottage, with blue walls that always made Fiona feel like she was under the sea in a beautiful cave with white wicker furniture. She was almost to the kitchen when Mrs. Lordeau called out, "See if you can get

Mayflower to come in here. Ever since my accident, he's been a bit nervous."

Mayflower was pacing by his food bowl. He was a dog the size of furniture, like a coffee table or a big-screen television. His giant paws pounded the floor, only stopping when he paused to sniff around his food bowl. Fiona put the food containers in the refrigerator and then stuck out her hand to Mayflower. "Good, good boy," said Fiona, scratching under his jowls. "Come on, let's go into the living room."

Mayflower paced some more, and Fiona watched him go back and forth in the kitchen until she began to feel dizzy. She grabbed a biscuit from the treat jar on the counter and held it out to Mayflower. Then she patted her leg. "Come on, boy. Let's go."

Mayflower closed his eyes and whined. But Fiona called his name once more, and when she patted her leg again, Mayflower followed.

"Mayflower!" said Mrs. Lordeau when Fiona and the dog came into the living room. Mayflower sniffed at Mrs. Miltenberger's knees before lying down in front of the couch. Mrs. Lordeau stroked his ears. "It's okay," she soothed. "It's okay." Then Mrs. Lordeau said to Fiona, "Poor thing is a ball of nerves. Just keeps pacing. How's your polly-wog?"

"No legs yet."

"Don't you worry about it, they'll come. They'll come. All in good time." She rubbed Mayflower's back with the toe of her good foot.

"I guess."

Mrs. Miltenberger cleared her throat, and Mrs. Lordeau said, "Right. Fiona, I've been doing some thinking. What do you say to walking Mayflower after school until my leg gets better? I think maybe getting him out of the house for some exercise would help calm him. At least I hope so. I'll pay you, of course."

Fiona couldn't believe her ears. She stood up and shouted, "Yes! Yes! That's what I say!"

Mrs. Miltenberger and Mrs. Lordeau laughed and Mayflower howled.

"Can I take him now?" asked Fiona.

"It'll be dark soon," said Mrs. Miltenberger. "Why don't you wait until tomorrow?"

"Just a short one?" Fiona said. "I won't go far."

Mayflower howled again. "Is that a 'yes,' boy?" Mrs. Lordeau said. Mayflower jumped up and ran in circles at her feet. "His leash is hanging by the kitchen door, Fiona."

Fiona ran to the kitchen, grabbed Mayflower's leash off the hook, and was back before Mrs. Miltenberger had gotten Mrs. Lordeau to her feet. "Try to stay away from other dogs," said Mrs. Lordeau. "Mayflower thinks he's a person, so he doesn't care too much for other dogs."

"Okay," said Fiona. "I will." She led Mayflower out the front door and onto the porch.

"Cats too!" hollered Mrs. Lordeau. "Best to just steer clear of all animals."

Fiona shouted back, "I will!" and then she and Mayflower were off down the street.

Mayflower's legs were almost as long as Fiona's, so keeping up with him was easy. Every now and then he looked up at Fiona, as if to say, *Thank you for getting me a change of scenery.* Fiona was excited too. How lucky she was that she came over to Mrs. Lordeau's, and how lucky that Mrs. Lordeau had an injured leg.

"We'll just go down the next street," Fiona told Mayflower. "And then I'll take you back home. But don't worry, we'll go on a longer walk tomorrow."

The pair followed the sidewalk onto Mulberry Street. Fiona let Mayflower sniff at whatever he found interesting, which turned out to be a lot. He found something really good underneath a holly tree and sniffed at it for a long time. After a while,

Fiona told him that they had to go, and she tugged on the leash. But he planted his enormous feet into the ground and pulled back at her.

"Mayflower," said Fiona. "What are you doing?"

At this point, Mayflower's head and half of his body had disappeared under the holly branches. Fiona held tight to the leash and got on all fours next to him. She lifted the branches and stuck her head in. It was dark under the leaves and prickly, too. She saw a gum wrapper and an empty juice box, but Fiona didn't think that was worth getting scratched up for.

Mayflower whined and pulled, but Fiona wouldn't let him go in any farther. She worried that if she let him go in another inch, they both would never get out. She tugged at the leash again, but Mayflower snorted and whined. "Mayflower, no!"

Then, just as Fiona was wondering how she got into this mess, something moved a few feet in front of her. Mayflower noticed it too, because a second later he turned around and bolted straight out of the holly tree. The sudden pull on the leash knocked Fiona off balance. She fell face-first into the dirt and rolled out onto the sidewalk.

Next to her, Mayflower spun in circles on his leash, whining. That's when Fiona saw a rabbit nibbling on clover nearby. "You're not supposed to do things like that," said Fiona, brushing the dirt off her clothes. Mayflower scratched at his ear. But Fiona wasn't ready to accept his apology. "For that, we're going home." She shortened the leash by wrapping it over her hand a few times and did not let Mayflower stop to get in one sniff for a whole entire block.

But then, as they were nearing Mrs. Lordeau's house, Fiona spotted the boy with the chicken. Actually, Mayflower spotted him first and howled. "Now what?" said Fiona, before she saw him. The boy was walking his chicken on a leash, just like before, only this time, the chicken wasn't out in front. He was walking behind.

"Hey there!" shouted Fiona. "Hey, wait up!" She tugged on Mayflower's leash and took off in a run toward the boy and his chicken.

The boy kept on walking, even as Fiona and Mayflower closed in. Fiona thought he seemed to be walking even faster. Mayflower continued to howl, and when they were only a few feet away, the boy scooped up the chicken into his arms and said, "What are you after?"

Fiona wasn't expecting that question. She wasn't after anything, really. "I've never seen anybody walk a chicken before."

The bird flapped its wings and Mayflower whined and jumped at it. The chicken boy held his hand out to Mayflower and said, "Hush there. Hushabye now."

"He doesn't like other animals too well," Fiona told him. But to her surprise, Mayflower got quiet. He even lay down. "How'd you do that?" asked Fiona.

But the chicken boy was already walking away. Fiona pulled at Mayflower's leash, but he wouldn't move. "Come on, Mayflower! What is wrong with you?" She pulled again, but it was like the boy put some kind of spell on him. Fiona yelled as the boy and his chicken disappeared down the street, "How do I undo this?!"

Fiona got on her knees and looked into Mayflower's big brown eyes. "Mrs. Miltenberger and

Mrs. Lordeau will be worrying about us if we don't get back soon. Don't you want to go on walks anymore?" She pulled at his collar, but all he did was yawn. "Fine," said Fiona. She went around to his rear end and gave him a push until most of his body was over his front legs. He finally got to his feet and Fiona pulled him the rest of the way home.

• Chapter 9 •

Fiona couldn't wait to tell everyone about her new job. Her mom didn't answer her phone, so Fiona left a message. "I have a job! I am a dog walker and the dog is named Mayflower and I walked him for the first time tonight and even got paid for it. Ten dollars, which may not be a lot, not as much as you make for being an actress, but it's something and a job is a job, so I can help out now that I have a job in case you lose yours. Call me back so I can also tell you about the chicken boy, who I've seen twice already and talked to once even though he isn't really friendly and he put a spell on—"

Her mom's phone cut Fiona off with a beep.

Talking about her new dog-walking job, even to her mom's answering machine, made her feel important. And taller even. Maybe that was how you knew you were a grown-up, she thought. You actually grew.

She had grown tall enough, in fact, that she now had to look down on Cleo, Milo, and Harold at school when she talked to them. "I've got important things to do," she said when Cleo asked her if she wanted to practice handing out maps after school.

"Like what?"

"I'm going to walk Mayflower. It's my job." This made Cleo roll her eyes. And Fiona said, "That's not a very grown-up thing to do."

Harold put his finger in his nose and said, "Somebody thinks she's pretty big and important today."

Fiona said, "When are you going to stop putting your finger up there?"

Harold pulled out his finger and wiped it under his desk. "Boise Idaho, you're mean."

Mr. Bland didn't seem to notice how grown up Fiona was. When he asked Milo to solve a word problem that involved two trains leaving the station at different times, Milo got it wrong, and Fiona said, "Oh, Milo. You should really study more."

Mr. Bland then said, "If you know so much, Fiona Finkelstein, then what's the right answer?"

Fiona didn't know the right answer and didn't understand why Mr. Bland was asking her about it, anyway. When she told him she didn't know, he said, "You should take your own advice and leave Milo alone."

But Fiona was too grown up, and too tall, to be bothered by all this. She was thinking about what everybody was going to say when she told them how she was going to California. Because she had figured that now that she wasn't a kid anymore, her dad couldn't tell her no.

Fiona couldn't wait for him to get home from work, so after school she went to WORD news station to ask. "Didn't we already have this conversation?" he said.

"But that was before."

Dad stared at weather maps on his computer screen. "Before what?"

"Before I was grown up enough," she said.

"It was last week."

"A lot can happen in a week," said Fiona. "Don't I look taller?" She backed up a few steps so he could get a good look at her.

Dad glanced up at her from his desk. "I guess so. But the answer is still no."

"But I'm a grown-up!" Fiona shouted, stomping her feet. "I am! I am!" As she yelled and hollered and as her dad just sat there, staring at her with wide eyes, somehow she didn't feel as tall. Was it possible to ungrow, too?

Chapter 10

Fiona walked Mayflower all over Ordinary. She was careful to watch out for rabbits and other animals, and she steered clear of holly bushes. Especially big ones that she could get dragged into and rolled out of.

On every walk, she looked for the chicken boy. He was just about as mysterious as Bigfoot, except not as big or hairy. Which made him hard to spot. She wondered what school he went to and what he did with the chicken while he was there all day. The spell he put on Mayflower only made Fiona want to find him more. A spell like that could really come in handy, and what she really wanted to know was, *Can you use it on teachers, and could you make it last more than a couple of minutes?*

After a few days of no sightings, Fiona finally saw the chicken boy again. He was walking along Baker's Park before sunset and sat down on a bench by the pond. Fiona watched as he scooped up the chicken and cradled it in his lap. This was Fiona's chance. She gave Mayflower's leash a strong pull and headed straight for them.

Mayflower managed to stay quiet until they were only a few steps away. Then he howled as loud as ever, and the boy and his chicken jumped. "Easy, girl," said the boy, stroking the bird's feathers. It clucked and stretched its wings. "There, there. Easy," he said. "Hush now. Hushabye." And just like that, the chicken settled into the boy's lap and was quiet.

Mayflower sniffed at the boy's legs and got face-to-face with the chicken. He howled. "Do you remember me?" said Fiona. "You put a spell on my dog the other day? Well, he's not really *my* dog. I don't have a dog, I have a pollywog. It's my job to walk him—the dog, I mean, not the pollywog. His name is Mayflower." She had to shout above all of Mayflower's howls.

The boy snapped his fingers at Mayflower then and said, "Hush now." Which was the same thing he said before that put Mayflower in a trance. Just like the last time, Mayflower lay down. And he rested his head on the boy's feet. "Hey," said Fiona. "How'd you do that?"

"Do what?"

Fiona pointed at Mayflower, who looked like he was about to fall asleep. "That."

The boy shrugged. "I just talk to animals like they understand what I'm saying."

"I've been talking to Mayflower here about not chasing rabbits, and he doesn't seem to understand *me*."

The boy scratched the chicken's head, and the bird clucked softly.

"I've never seen anybody walk a chicken before," said Fiona.

"You can walk almost anything," said the boy.

"Not a pollywog."

He bit his lip like he was thinking that maybe you could walk a pollywog. If they had legs to walk on. But all he said was, "Flo here likes sunsets. Best views are here and over by the old fountain."

Fiona pointed to the chicken. "This is Flo?" Flo clucked and stretched her neck, as if to say, *The one and only.* Pride was a quality Fiona had to admire in a chicken.

Fiona sat down on the bench next to the chicken boy and introduced herself.

"Tom," said the boy, his eyes still on the sky.

Fiona had a lot of questions in her head that were itching to get out. "How old are you? Do you go to school around here?"

"Thirteen," said Tom. "South Jefferson Middle."

"I go to Ordinary Elementary," she said. "How come I never saw you before?"

"Maybe you have."

"Nope," said Fiona, shaking her head. "There's a lot of ordinary in Ordinary, and somebody walking a chicken on a leash is something I definitely would've remembered."

He scrunched up his face. "What's that supposed to mean?"

"Nothing," said Fiona. "Just that it's not every day you see a chicken boy."

"Don't call me a—"

"We could start an animal-walking business," said Fiona. "I'm trying to get enough money to go to California. The more animals we have, the more money we could make. What do you think?"

"No thanks," said Tom.

"Why not?"

But Tom didn't say why not. He didn't say anything else at all. He just stared at the sky.

Fiona watched awhile too, watched the orange burn bright and fade into pink and then disappear altogether. She had another question. "How long are we going to sit here and look at this for?"

"You can sit here as long as you like," he said. "It's a public park." Then he nodded toward Flo. "We're here until Flo's ready to go."

"To go where?" said Fiona.

Again, nothing. The more questions she asked,

the less she found out. Finally Tom had a question of his own. "What do you feed him?"

Fiona looked at Mayflower, who was snoring. "I don't feed him. My job is just to take him on walks."

Tom shook his head. "Your pollywog is what I mean. You do feed him, don't you?"

"Oh. Mr. Funbucket eats boiled lettuce mostly. We're still waiting on his legs to arrive."

Tom nodded, and as he did, Flo stood on his lap. Right away, he gently put his arm around her belly and lowered her to the ground. Flo leaned over to where Mayflower was lying and stuck her beak in his ear. This must have been enough to undo Mayflower's spell, because he raised his head and started to bark. Fiona's heart started racing. She pulled at Mayflower's leash. There was no way she would let him have chicken for dinner tonight.

"What should I do?" said Fiona.

"About what?" said Tom.

"Mayflower wants to eat Flo!"

Tom laughed. "He's just talking to her."

Flo stretched her neck at Mayflower and continued pecking at his ear. For being a chicken, Flo sure was brave.

Tom clucked his tongue and gathered the end of Flo's leash into his hand. "Come on, stop riling that old dog." He took a few steps and then turned back to Fiona and Mayflower, who was standing up and barking with such force that Fiona worried his teeth might rattle loose. "Hold out your hand like this." He showed her with his own hand, held flat with his palm to the ground.

Fiona made her hand look like his. "Now hold it above his head, back a little," he said. Right away, Mayflower looked up and stopped barking. And when his head went up, his rear end went down. "Now, lower your hand real slow," Tom said.

Fiona did, and when Mayflower lay down, Fiona got so excited she yelled, "I did the spell! I did the spell!" She scratched Mayflower's chin and said, "Did you see?" But Tom and Flo were already down the path, walking toward the sunset.

Fiona, and when Miltenberger, Fiona
got so she did she did the
spell. She scratched May flower's chin and said,
"Did you and Tom already down
the path, we

Chapter 11

iona peered into the bowl and examined Mr. Funbucket. He was still just a fish, and Fiona was beginning to wonder if Rick from the pet store had sold her a lemon of a pollywog.

"A watched pot never boils," said Mrs. Miltenberger.

"What does that mean?" asked Fiona.

"It means staring at that pollywog all night won't make it grow legs."

Fiona wondered if the chicken boy knew a spell for sprouting pollywog legs. Max leapt off the couch and landed practically on top of Fiona.

"Hey!" said Fiona.

"Do you want to buy a sticker?" asked Max.

"No way."

"Half price."

Fiona shook her head.

"I made it special just for you," he said. "And I promise this one is really nice."

"Let's see it."

Max grinned and pulled a handful of stickers from the pocket of his swim trunks. He sifted through them and then held one out to Fiona. Written on it were these words: I LOVE MAX.

Fiona tossed it back to him. "No thanks."

He handed her another sticker. "How about one that says 'Max Is the Best'?" Fiona sighed. "I've got a whole bunch about how great Captain Seahorse is."

Fiona held her hands out, just above Max's head. "Hushabye," she said. "Hush."

Max looked up, and when he did, he stopped talking. Fiona lowered her hand slowly until Max sat cross-legged on the floor. "What are you doing?"

"Hush. Hush now," Fiona said, trying to make her voice as gentle as the chicken man's.

Max stared up at her, and Fiona smiled at the same bewilderment in his eyes that she'd seen in Mayflower's. So the spell worked on people, too. This was very good to know. "Stay," she said to Max. "Good boy."

Fiona found Tom and Flo sitting on the same park bench the next evening. Before Fiona had a chance to use her spell on Mayflower, he stopped barking and settled at Tom's feet. Fiona sat next to Tom. "The spell works on people," she told him. "Six-year-old boy people, at least."

"Spell?" said Tom. He scratched Flo's head with the tip of his pointer finger.

"The magic trick you showed me on Mayflower. Do you know any more?"

Tom shook his head, but Fiona wasn't sure she believed him. In fact, she was sure she didn't. "Why does Flo walk on a leash like a dog?"

Tom stroked Flo's feathers, and after a while said, "She thinks she is one."

"One what?"

"A dog." Flo clucked in agreement.

"Why does she think that?"

Tom said, "She was raised with a dog. I guess she never could see any difference between them."

"Maybe you should get her a mirror so she can see what a chicken looks like," Fiona said.

He scratched his head. "Won't help. She wants to be something she's not."

Fiona gently touched Flo's wing. She flat-out understood that kind of thinking. "You should enter her in the fair or something. I bet you could get a prize because no one has ever seen a chicken like her before."

Tom shrugged.

"So you're going to enter her?" said Fiona.

"Nope."

"Why not? Don't you want to win a prize?"

"Nope."

"I never met a person who didn't want to win a prize or be noticed for something," said Fiona. This was a first.

"Now you have," said Tom.

Then two boys walked right by where Fiona and Tom were sitting. They looked to be about Tom's age, and Fiona wasn't sure, but she thought she saw Tom grip Flo's leash a little tighter.

The boys said something in low voices, so low Fiona couldn't make it out, and then they laughed.

After they passed, Fiona was going to ask Tom about what other tricks Flo could do. But before she had a chance, Tom said, "Why are you following me all the time, anyway?"

Fiona wasn't expecting that question, and she didn't know what to say. All of a sudden she felt like she was doing something wrong by sitting here. "Because we're both walkers," she finally said.

"So?"

"And because everybody could use some company."

"Who told you that?"

"Mrs. O'Brien."

"Well, I don't want any." Then he muttered something, but Flo happened to cluck at the same time, and Fiona couldn't hear what Tom said. He reached down and patted Mayflower on the back. "Nice boy," he said.

One thing was clear to Fiona: Tom liked Mayflower a lot more than he liked her. "Don't you want my company?"

Mayflower rolled over onto his back so Tom could scratch his stomach. Tom pressed his lips together like he was trying to keep words inside. Eventually he stopped petting Mayflower. Then he looked away from Fiona and said, "You're a kid."

"So are you," she said. After all, Tom was only a couple of years older.

"Not so much as you."

Fiona felt her hands tighten into fists. "I am not. Kids don't have jobs, and I have a job."

Tom shook his head. "A job doesn't make you a grown-up."

"Yes, it does."

"No, it doesn't."

"Yes, it does." Fiona stood up. "Come on, Mayflower. Let's go." But that dog stayed where he was. "Come on, Mayflower. I said we're going." She tugged at his leash.

"Mayflower," said Tom in a low voice. And don't you know that Mayflower stood right up and looked at Tom as though Fiona wasn't even there. Something else was becoming clear: Mayflower didn't think of Fiona as a grown-up one bit. Not when Tom was around, at least.

• Chapter 12 •

Fiona stared into the fishbowl. "He's depressed," she told Mrs. Miltenberger.

"Who is?"

"Mr. Funbucket," said Fiona.

Mrs. Miltenberger put down her crossword puzzle and said, "How can you tell?"

Fiona stuck her finger in the water and made a little splash, just to give Mr. Funbucket some excitement. "All he does is swim around and around."

"I hate to break it to you, kiddo," said Mrs. Miltenberger, "but that's what fish do."

Fiona wasn't convinced. "He could be crying right now, and we wouldn't even know."

Mrs. Miltenberger sighed and then turned the television to the local news. "Your father's weather forecast is coming on."

Fiona leaned in close to the bowl and whispered into the water. "Mr. Funbucket," she said, "I don't know what you're waiting for, but you'll be a lot happier once you get your legs." Then she got up to go to her room.

"Aren't you going to stay and watch your father?" asked Mrs. Miltenberger.

Fiona shook her head. The weather, she figured, wouldn't change things.

It rained for the next three days, so Fiona didn't walk Mayflower. And she didn't see Tom or Flo. If dogs didn't like the rain, she guessed chickens didn't either.

Meanwhile, at school, nobody else seemed to believe there really was a chicken boy.

"I want to see the chicken boy," said Harold after school. He zipped up his book bag and slung it on his back. "I told my grandma all about him and she didn't believe me. She wants proof."

"Me too," said Cleo. "It's no fair that you get him all to yourself."

"Unless there really isn't a chicken boy at all," said Milo.

Fiona dropped her Thinking Pencil into her tote bag. "Fine," she told them. "You can come to Baker's Park later and see for yourself."

On the walk to Mrs. Lordeau's, Fiona wondered if Tom and Flo would even be at the park. And what would Cleo and Harold and Milo say if he wasn't there.

At Mrs. Lordeau's house, Mayflower was waiting at the door. "Thank heavens the rain has finally stopped," said Mrs. Lordeau. "He's been a wreck these last few days. Nervous, scratchy even. These walks are so good for him, Fiona.

When he misses them, he really misses them."

Fiona led Mayflower down the porch steps and started their regular route toward the park. Mayflower took the lead, pulling Fiona along. "Slow down," she told him. She wasn't in a hurry to get to where they were going. "Let's go someplace else today. I'm tired of the park." She pulled on Mayflower's leash and started walking toward downtown Ordinary.

Mayflower seemed confused at first. He grabbed part of the leash in his mouth and pulled, as if to say, *You're going the wrong way!*

"Tom doesn't want company," Fiona told him. "At least, he doesn't want me hanging around." Mayflower barked. "I know, Harold and Cleo and Milo will be there waiting for us. I know." Mayflower whined and scratched his ear. Fiona sighed and looked down at the slobbering dog. "Mayflower, from now on it's just you and me."

As they walked, Fiona wondered how you could

try so hard to get somewhere and never get even close. She had tried her best to be a grown-up, done everything she knew how, but no matter how good of a dog walker she was, she was still just a fourth grader to the chicken boy, to her dad, and to everyone else.

When Mayflower stopped to drink out of a fountain on the corner of Second Street, two boys came up to them. The very same ones she saw at the park. "I know you," one of them said. "You hang out with that guy who thinks he's a chicken." The other boy laughed. He had awful teeth.

You don't know me, Fiona wanted to say. *Not at all.* But instead she just said, "Tom doesn't think he's a chicken."

"That's right," said the boy. "He just *wants* to be a chicken."

Then they started making high-pitched noises at each other and at Fiona, noises that Fiona knew were supposed to sound like a chicken but really didn't at all. Mayflower must have thought so too, because he stopped drinking and lifted his front legs off the ground. Then he howled. That shut the boys up pretty good, and they looked back over their shoulders a couple of times as they crossed the street.

"Good boy," said Fiona, scratching Mayflower's ears.

Fiona and Mayflower walked on. She didn't think that Tom really wanted to be a chicken, like those boys said, but she hoped that he did, in a way, because it was nice to know that other people besides her wanted to be something that they weren't.

A while later, Fiona found herself in front of The Fish Hut. She peered in the window, and Mayflower stood on his hind legs and licked at the glass door. There was Rick. Fiona watched as he scooped out a pollywog for a customer and dumped it into a plastic bag.

All at once, Fiona felt her face get hot. She scratched at her cheek. It was one thing to not give Fiona a job, but it was another thing—a much more despicable thing—to sell her a lemon of a pollywog. She started to push open the door, but this time she read the sign. It read NO PETS ALLOWED INSIDE. This made no sense at all to Fiona because the whole entire store was nothing but pets!

She looked at Mayflower and then looked around to find someplace to put him while she was inside. There was a tree in front of the store next to The Fish Hut. "I'll only be a minute, Mayflower." She wrapped his leash around the trunk of the tree and looped it through in a knot. "You stay here, and I'll be right back."

Inside The Fish Hut, the tanks were bubbling and giving off a quiet hum. She said a quick hello to the tank of pollywogs near the register; after all, they were Mr. Funbucket's brothers and sisters, and probably cousins even. She checked for legs (there weren't any) and then stood before Rick. "Remember me?" she said.

He looked Fiona over. "Ah, the fish rouser. How's your pollywog?"

"Still swimming," she said.

"Good."

Fiona shook her head. "Not so good. It's a lemon. Mr. Funbucket wants to be a frog. He is supposed to be a frog by now. But he doesn't have any legs."

"They'll come," said Rick. "All pollywogs eventually get their legs. You just need to gain some patience."

"How can you be so sure he's not a lemon?" asked Fiona.

Two customers started to lurk nearby. Fiona could tell they were listening.

Rick said in a loud voice, "There are no lemons in The Fish Hut. That is a guarantee."

Fiona made sure the other customers heard her

when she said, "You mean if Mr. Funbucket doesn't sprout legs, I can get my money back?"

Rick cleared his throat. "That's The Fish Hut promise."

"Okay," said Fiona with a smile. "A promise is a promise." A satisfied customer, Fiona headed for the door. As she pushed it open, she thought of one more thing. She turned to Rick. "I think you should let pets in here, on account of the fact that you have pets in here already, and you could probably get more customers."

Rick rubbed his chin and laughed. "Still looking for a job, are you now?"

"No," said Fiona. "I have a job. I'm a dog walker. As a matter of fact, I'm working right now. He's right out . . ." Fiona pointed outside at Mayflower. But the spot under the tree where she left him was empty! "Mayflower!"

Fiona pushed open the door and raced outside. "Mayflower!" she shouted again. Fiona began to sweat. She ran up and down the street calling his name. But there was no answer and no Mayflower.

She fought back tears when she stopped to catch her breath. Her legs ached, and she didn't know what to do or where else to look. Then she remembered that Harold and Cleo and Milo were waiting for her somewhere in Baker's Park. After all, she needed help. Mayflower needed help.

She got her legs going again and ran all the way to the park without stopping.

Fiona raced through the park's entrance. She weaved her way around park-goers. "Excuse me! Watch out, please!" she shouted. No one else seemed to be in the least bit of a hurry. Apparently Fiona was the only person in Ordinary who was frantically looking for a runaway dog.

She took a shortcut across the footbridge toward the clock tower. She didn't want to think about all the awful things that could have happened to Mayflower. Was he dog-napped? What if he had wandered into the street and been hit by a car? Fiona shook her head to scatter the thoughts.

Finally the clock tower came into view and Fiona ran straight for it. Her legs were rubber, but she couldn't stop because if she did, she was sure she would never get them going again. When she reached the tower, Fiona fell to her knees in the grass. She held her side where a cramp had started and searched for any signs of her friends.

They were nowhere. Fiona's stomach gurgled and sank. What had she done?

So tired, her eyes filled up. She would have to tell Mrs. Lordeau. How would she tell Mrs. Lordeau? And then, from somewhere nearby, she heard someone call her name. She listened, looked around, and there behind her stood Cleo, Harold, and Milo.

Fiona wiped her eyes and got to her feet. She leaned on Cleo and hugged her.

"Where have you been?" said Milo. "We've been waiting all this time."

Cleo asked, "Are you okay? You don't look so good."

Fiona shook her head.

"I brought my camera," said Harold. "Where's the chicken boy?"

When Fiona caught her breath, she told them, "I need your help."

Chapter 13

Fiona and her friends decided to split up and search the streets of Ordinary for Mayflower. Fiona would search the park, too tired to go any farther. "He's got brown hair and very tall legs and sad eyes that make you want to say you're sorry even if you don't have a reason to."

"Is his hair more of a light brown like sand or dark brown like chocolate?" asked Harold.

"Brown like dirt," said Fiona.

"Like dirt that's dry or dirt that's wet?"

Fiona snapped, "Harold, just brown. Brown. He's a brown dog!"

"I'm just trying to get a good picture of what Mayflower looks like so I'll know him when I see him," said Harold. "You don't have to be so mean."

Fiona said she was sorry. "I'm just worried is all."

Cleo patted Fiona's arm. "If we see a dog that's by itself, without an owner, no matter what kind of brown it is, we should probably just get it. You know, to be safe."

"Sounds like a plan," said Milo. He pointed to the clock on the tower. "It's six o'clock. Everybody meets back here in an hour. With or without a brown dog."

Fiona watched Cleo, Harold, and Milo take off in opposite directions. She was on her own again. After taking a deep breath, she continued looking for Mayflower. There were lots of dogs at the park, but none was the dog she was missing.

As the sun began to set, Fiona found herself by the pond. Tom and Flo's bench was empty, and Fiona thought that she must have been such a bother that Tom decided to watch the sunset from some other spot just so she wouldn't find them. She lay down on the bench and stared up at the orange sky.

Tom was right: It was a good view from here. And then Fiona remembered. There was another place where Tom said you could see the sunset. She sat up with a spark and flew off the bench. She followed the path all the way to the other end of the park. The old fountain was three tiers tall and at the topmost tier, a metal fish spouted water from its puckered lips.

And in front of the fountain, a bench. Fiona gasped when she saw who was there. "Mayflower!" She raced to the bench and dove to the ground, where Mayflower was asleep at Tom's feet. "Where have you been?"

Mayflower yawned and licked Fiona's face like he was wondering what took her so long to get there. "I've been looking everywhere for you!"

Fiona cradled Mayflower's head in her arms, then got to her feet. Flo let out a cluck and then hopped down from Tom's lap to nestle in beside Mayflower's front paws. "They're friends," said Fiona.

Tom nodded. "Guess so."

They watched people at the park for a while. Every now and then someone came up to Tom and asked about Flo. When Tom was quiet, Fiona covered for him and explained that Flo walks on a leash because she thinks she's a dog.

"Maybe Flo knows she's a chicken but wants to be a dog," Fiona said to Tom.

"Maybe," he said.

Right about then a woman came up to them, handed them a flyer, and said, "The Great Ordinary Fair is Ordinary's biggest event. You don't want to miss it!"

Fiona looked at the flyer and groaned. "The only thing I'm going to miss is having any fun at the fair when I'm handing out maps to nobody and staring at a bunch of flowers." She handed the flyer to Tom. "You should enter Flo."

"I'm working the poultry pavilion," said Tom. "Can't enter Flo. That would be against the rules."

"The poultry pavilion?"

Flo clucked and Tom nodded. "The Ordinary Humane Society; that's where I volunteer. This year they put me in charge of fowls."

"At least it's not maps."

"I guess," he said. "I wanted to be in charge of the alpaca center. But since I have a chicken, that's where they put me. There's always next year, I suppose."

"That's what everybody tells me all the time," said Fiona. "After they say no."

Tom leaned back on the bench and sighed.

Flo nested against Mayflower and scratched his belly with her beak. Mayflower pushed at Flo with his paw and then whined. "Who ever heard of a dog being friends with a chicken?"

"Not me," said Tom.

"Me neither."

Humane Society; that's where I volunteer. This year they put me in charge of the

"At least I hope—"

"I guess so. I want to, but that's not of the dispenser, but since I have chickens, that's where they put me. There's always next year, I suppose."

○ Chapter 14 ○

Fiona led Mayflower through the park to the clock tower, where Milo, Cleo, and Harold were waiting.

"Is that Mayflower?" said Cleo, running over to her. "Where did you find him?"

"He was with Flo," said Fiona. "I guess he wanted to watch the sunset with them."

Harold bent down and looked at Mayflower. "You said he was brown! He's not brown. He's red!"

Cleo cracked her knuckles. "Oh, Harold."

Milo took a step toward Fiona. "Okay, where's the chicken boy?"

Fiona pointed to the other end of the park. "Over there."

"Let's go," said Milo.

"It's going to be dark soon," said Fiona. "And I have to get Mayflower back to Mrs. Lordeau's house."

"Then we'll go," said Milo.

Cleo said, "I have to get to the restaurant. My mom and dad will be wondering where I am."

"Fine," said Milo. "Harold and me will go."

"He won't be there." Fiona pointed to the small band of orange left in the sky. "They only stay for the sunset."

Harold gripped his camera and moaned. "Grandma is going to be really disappointed. Now I'll have to let her win at Scrabble so I won't feel so guilty."

"Sorry," said Fiona. "I guess you'll have to meet him another time."

"If there really is a chicken boy," said Milo.

Fiona smiled and shrugged.

After school the next day, the Bingo Broads were waiting for Fiona in the parking lot. Mrs. O'Brien was in the driver's seat, and Mrs. Miltenberger, Mrs. Huff, and Mrs. Lordeau were in the back.

"How's my girl?" said Mrs. Miltenberger.

"Fine and dandy," said Fiona. But then she saw Mrs. Lordeau's foot. "Where's the boot?"

"Gone for good," said Mrs. Lordeau. "We just came from the doctor's. She said that my leg is healing up lovely. So lovely that I don't need that ugly old boot any longer." She looked at her bare foot stuffed into a flip-flop. "Toes, oh, how I've missed seeing you."

Fiona smiled as Mrs. Lordeau wiggled her toes.

"So," said Mrs. Miltenberger quietly. She put her hand on Fiona's knee. "Mrs. Lordeau will be able to walk Mayflower from now on."

"Oh," said Fiona when she understood what that meant: that *she* wouldn't be walking Mayflower from now on.

"I'm sorry, lovey," said Mrs. Lordeau. "But the doctor wants me to get as much exercise as I can now. To get back my strength. And you knew this was only temporary, right?"

Fiona nodded. It was hard not to feel like she fell right on her face.

"Maybe this afternoon you could show me where you take Mayflower," said Mrs. Lordeau. "How does that sound?"

Fiona swallowed hard. "Sounds fine." Only it flat-out didn't.

"You handled that very well," said Mrs. Miltenberger to Fiona when they got home. "I know you're disappointed that you don't have your dog-walking job anymore, so it was good of you to be so nice about it when Mrs. Lordeau told you."

Fiona checked on Mr. Funbucket. He was as much of a fish as ever. She sighed. "Even though I wouldn't want this to happen, do you think one day she might slip and hurt her other leg and I'll get to walk Mayflower again?"

"Fiona!"

"I said that I wouldn't want it to happen." If there was the slightest chance that someday, sometime in the future, she might be able to get her job back, then it would make her feel a little bit less awful. And that eventually, someday, she would be closer to being a grown-up.

Mrs. Miltenberger smiled. "I suppose there is a chance. Considering how clumsy she is. But don't tell her I said that."

"Okay," said Fiona.

"Does that help?"

Fiona nodded. "A little."

"Tell you what," said Mrs. Miltenberger. "I'll drive you over to Mrs. Lordeau's. And maybe we'll swing by the creamery for a milk shake."

• Chapter 15 •

The day before the grand opening of the Great Ordinary Fair, Mr. Bland's class took a school bus to the fairgrounds. They unloaded at the front gate. Fiona got off the bus and stared at the giant O of the Ferris wheel at the center of the fair. Cars poured through the gate and people rushed about setting up food stands, arts-and-crafts booths, and games.

"Cheer up," said Cleo. "We're out of school and at the fair."

Fiona couldn't help it. She felt lousy about

having to give out maps to nobody and about not having a job anymore. And she really missed seeing Mayflower and Flo and Tom.

Cleo took a deep breath. "Do you smell that?"

"What?" said Harold.

"Fair food," said Cleo. "Like funnel cakes and corn dogs. Yum."

"Where are all the animals?" said Milo.

Cleo pointed to the other end of the fairgrounds, beyond the Ferris wheel. "All the way over there."

"There's even a birthing station over there, where you can see animals get born," said Fiona. "That's where I wanted my map station to be."

"Whoa," said Milo. "Cool."

Harold shook his head. "That's what I thought last year, until I saw a cow have a cow. And I almost lost my corn dog."

Mr. Bland said, "Gather around, people. Gather around."

Cleo grabbed Fiona's hand, and they huddled around Mr. Bland.

He pulled a rubber band off a stack of paper and then handed the pages to Harold. "Take one and pass them along. These are your map stations, in case you've forgotten where you've been assigned. You and your partners are to go to your station and get familiar with what's nearby. We're doing this so that there won't be any confusion tomorrow when the fair is open to the public. There will be enough going on here, so I want

everybody to know exactly where they are supposed to be. Got it?"

"Got it," everybody said.

"Stay with your partner." Mr. Bland looked at his
watch. "I want you all back here in fifteen minutes."

Cleo squeezed Fiona's hand.

"On your mark, get set, go," said Mr. Bland. And
everybody took off in different directions.

"Let's go," said Fiona, pulling on Cleo's arm.
"This way." They made their way past the games,
past the carnival rides, past the tractors and flower
sellers, and all the way to no-man's-land. Fiona
pointed to their station when it came into view.
"There's Bridget's Mums," she said.

"I'm hungry," said Cleo. "There's a pretzel stand
over there. Want to split one?"

Fiona nodded and dug in her pocket for some
change. Cleo went off to the pretzel stand, and
then Fiona remembered. "No mustard," she called
to her. And then Fiona's feet stopped. Down at

the other end of the food vendors, she spotted a chicken in a crowd of people. Not a chicken turning on a skewer all cooked and barbecued, but one with feathers, alive, and walking around on a leash. "Flo!"

Fiona ran toward her. She raced past the food stands, dodging workers putting up tents and firing outdoor ovens. She kept her eyes on Flo. The crowd parted as Fiona got closer, and there was Tom. His back was to Fiona as he started to lead Flo away.

Fiona shouted, "Wait!" as she ran. Tom and Flo seemed to turn around at the same time, and as soon as Tom saw who was shouting, he picked up Flo and braced her with his arm.

"Saw you coming," said Tom.

Fiona gently smoothed her fingers over Flo's back and wings. Flo tucked her head under her wing. "What's the matter, girl? Aren't you happy to see me?"

Tom cupped his hand over Flo's head. "I'm worried about her. She's not eating. Won't even take food out of my hand." He shook his head and chewed on his lip. "Something's wrong, I just know it."

"She's sick?"

"I don't know," he said. "Something's not right." He hugged Flo tight to him and nuzzled her feathers with his nose. "I've got to get back."

Fiona watched as they disappeared into the crowd.

• Chapter 16 •

wish I could go to the fair today," said Max, after gargling his orange juice and spitting it back into his glass.

"Don't do that again," said Mrs. Miltenberger. "And you'll get to go next year when you're in second grade."

"It's not as fun as you think when you have to work there," said Fiona, poking at her scrambled eggs.

"You mean like having a job?" said Mrs. Miltenberger, smirking. "I thought someone *wanted* a job."

"Who?" said Max. "Who wanted a job?"

"Beats me," said Fiona. "I don't know who that was."

In the first hour of the Great Ordinary Fair, Fiona and Cleo handed out only one map. Nobody came to that end of the fairgrounds. Why would they? Except to haul a mum all over the place, and nobody wanted to do that.

"This is terrible," said Fiona.

Cleo cracked her knuckles. "At least we're not in school."

Fiona knew Cleo had a point. But still. "Hey, I've got an idea. Let's make paper airplanes and see whose flies the farthest."

She and Cleo each folded a map into a paper airplane. Cleo made tiny tears on the wings and held hers above her head when she finished. "My plane's got special wings."

"You go first," said Fiona.

Cleo spit on her fingers and then worked the nose of the airplane into a sharp point. "Okay. Here goes." She cocked her arm and then sprang the plane forward. The plane sailed through the air, catching some wind, and then did a nosedive into the side of a trash can.

"Good one." Fiona readied her plane and blew on it for good luck. Then she brought her arm back and launched the plane forward. Her plane took off and soared. Right into the stomach of Mr. Bland.

Mr. Bland picked up the plane, turned it over, and handed it back to Fiona. "This belongs to you?"

"Sorry," said Fiona. "It wasn't supposed to hit you in the stomach."

"Where was it supposed to hit me, then?" said Mr. Bland. But before he let Fiona answer, he said, "Never mind. Girls, when I said our class was going to hand out maps, I did not mean by throwing them at people."

"Sorry," Fiona said again.

"Yeah, sorry," said Cleo.

"I came to tell you that you can take a break for lunch," he said. "You've got an hour."

"But nobody comes back here," said Fiona. "We've only given away one map!"

"Then you might just have to try harder," he said as he walked away.

"Lunchtime," said Cleo.

Fiona's stomach grumbled. "Just in time."

"What do you want?" said Cleo. She pointed to a food stand at the end of their path. "I think that's a hot dog stand over there."

Fiona shook her head. "Chicken."

"What?"

"I want to go see how Flo is doing." Fiona looked at her map and quickly found the Poultry Pavilion. She took off at a run and weaved in and out of the crowds. She ran past the Ordinary Ferris wheel, past the games, past the tractors, and past the birthing center. The Poultry Pavilion was easy to spot. It had a giant metal chicken sitting on the roof. The door was propped open with a brick. She ducked inside.

The Poultry Pavilion was packed full of birds—hens, roosters, and turkeys, all in metal cages. Fiona had never seen so many birds in one place before. Some were all white, some were all black, and some looked just like Flo—brown with a red comb on top of their heads.

Tom was perched on a wooden stool in the corner. In a room full of chickens, Fiona thought he would be in chicken heaven, but something was wrong. She looked around. "Where's Flo?"

Tom shook his head. "I had to leave her at home."

"You left her at home?"

He put his head in his hands. "I don't know what's wrong. She's never been like this before. Never before."

Fiona tried to cheer him up. "She'll be okay. Last month I had the stomach flu and didn't want to eat anything for an entire day. And then when I felt better, I ate a whole pizza all by myself."

"I shouldn't have left her alone. I've never left her alone before. She won't know what's going on. She's got to be wondering where I am." Tom stood up. "Fiona, I need you to do me a big favor. I need you to watch over these birds while I go home and check on Flo."

It was the Mayflower incident all over again. "But I can't!"

"Then I'll just have to go."

"But won't you get in trouble?" said Fiona. "You're supposed to be in charge of the Poultry Pavilion."

"I've got to go see about Flo." Tom headed for the door.

"Okay," said Fiona. "I'll do it. I'll watch them. But you're coming back, right?"

"I'll be right back." Tom looked at the big clock on the wall above the door. "The birds are being judged in an hour, but I'll be back way before then. I just need to check to make sure Flo's okay."

"I have to be back at my map station in an hour," she told him.

"Then we're good," he said. "Look, all you have to do is just watch them."

"Easy peasy," Fiona said.

• Chapter 17 •

Only five minutes had passed since Tom left, but when all there was to do was stare at chickens in cages, five minutes seemed like a gazillion years. Especially when all of the chickens started looking at Fiona in a way that made Fiona think they wanted something.

Hundreds of tiny black beady eyes wouldn't stop staring at her. Fiona figured that the birds didn't understand why they were stuck in these cages, all cooped up with no room to run or explore. It wasn't their fault they were chickens, after all.

The more they stared at her, the more Fiona got to thinking. The chickens probably felt like everybody was against them. What they needed was for someone to be on their side. They just wanted to be able to do something on their own, like go to

California, or not even that so much. They just wanted people to stop saying no all the time just because they were chickens. All they wanted was to hear a yes once in a while. That's all!

Fiona knelt beside the chicken closest to her. The hen's short body was covered in long white feathers, and she had a tuft of white feathers that stood straight up on her head like a hat. The chicken rested its head against the side of the cage and was nearly eye-to-eye with Fiona. "I know. It's no fun being in a cage." She scratched its head, and the chicken clucked. Fiona looked at the tag tied around the chicken's ankle: PP072539. The number matched the tag clipped to the top of the cage. "Don't you have a name?"

PP072539 ruffled its feathers.

"You want out of there for a minute?" asked Fiona.

The chicken clucked again and inched toward her.

Fiona slid open the latch on the cage and opened the door. Right away the bird stuck out its head and took two steps out of the cage. It strutted around the floor. "There now," said Fiona. "It feels good to have some room to move around, doesn't it?"

The bird pecked at the concrete floor. That's what Flo did when she was hungry. Tom didn't tell her that she had to feed them. Fiona looked around the pavilion. She spotted a burlap grain bag leaning against a wall. The top of the bag was open, and Fiona sank her hands into the feed. She brought what she could carry over to the chicken and scattered it onto the floor.

The chicken attacked the grain. "You were hungry!" As soon as the feed hit the floor, all of the other birds flapped their wings and stuck their heads through the openings in their cages. They squawked and shrilled at Fiona. "Feed me feed me feed me feed me!" they cried.

Fiona didn't know what to do. Tom wasn't back

from checking on Flo, but all of the birds seemed hungry. Really hungry. Then she remembered how Tom talked to Flo like she was a person. She stood on top of the wooden stool. "Hello, hens! And also roosters and turkeys! Hello!" she said to them. "I need you all to listen to me!"

The birds quieted.

"Thank you," said Fiona. "Now I know you're hungry. But Tom didn't say anything about feeding you all while he was away. He'll be back real soon. He will! And then he'll take care of feeding you. Until then, everybody just needs to have some patience."

The birds made a racket. They hollered and knocked their wings into the cages. Apparently they did not like what Fiona had to say one bit.

"It's going to be okay," said Fiona. "I promise!" But she doubted that the chickens could hear her over all the noise they were making. Fiona looked at the clock. Thirty minutes had passed, and there was no sign of Tom anywhere. She put her hands over her ears and turned her back on them. If she didn't see or hear them, she could pretend they were all sleeping quietly in their cages. Only, the noises they made were so loud that even putting her hands over her ears didn't help.

Finally Fiona couldn't take it anymore. "You win!" She dragged the bag of feed to the middle of the room and kicked it over so that the grain spilled onto the ground. Then she opened the cages one by one. The birds flocked to the food and began to eat. Once all the birds were out of their cages, the room got quiet. Fiona watched as the birds happily pecked at their food. Some little chickens had a hard time getting around the big ones to find the food, so she helped them push their way through the crowd. "Hurry up and eat," she told them. "I've got to get you back in your cages before the judges come around."

When some of them looked like they were done

eating, Fiona bent down to scoop one up, just like she had done with Flo, to get her back in her cage. But she wasn't like Flo at all. She didn't like to be scooped. At least, not by Fiona. A red one puffed herself up so that she was almost twice her regular size and came at Fiona with wings flapping. The bird even screeched at Fiona and tried to peck her arm. Fiona was scared, but she had to get these chickens back in their cages.

She tried another one. A smaller bird this time. "Ow!" yelled Fiona when the bird bit her thumb. "What's wrong with you all? I gave you food and let you out! We had a deal!"

● Chapter 18 ●

Fiona pleaded with the chickens. "Come on, chicky chickies. Let's go back into your cages." She even threw some food into the cages to lure them in, but the chickens weren't falling for that old trick. "Where is Tom?"

The door to the pavilion swung open. "Fiona!" said Cleo. "What are you doing?"

"I don't know!" Fiona scratched her cheek. "They won't go back in their cages!"

"What are they doing out of them?"

"They were hungry. And noisy. I mean, really, really noisy."

"I'll go get somebody to help," said Cleo, turning back toward the door.

"No!" said Fiona. "Tom said he would be back before the judges come. He'll get in trouble if they find out he left."

"You're going to get in trouble if Mr. Bland finds out. We're supposed to be handing out maps, not playing Duck Duck Goose."

"I know that, Cleo," said Fiona. "And these are chickens, not ducks."

"What time are the judges coming?" asked Cleo.

Fiona picked up a chicken with long black feathers. "Two o'clock."

"That's in ten minutes!" shouted Cleo.

Fiona put the chicken into a cage and locked it. "Hey, I got one in!"

"Great," said Cleo. "Only a billion more to go." She picked up a bird, a big red one, and held it out away from her body. "What do I do with it now?"

Fiona said, "Put it into a cage before it bites you!"

"Which cage?"

"Any cage!"

Then Cleo yelled, "Yeeeeooow! Too late!" She dropped the chicken and sucked on her finger where it was bitten. "What are we going to do now?"

Just then, the door to the pavilion opened. Tom yelled, "Blasted! Fiona, what did you do?"

"I had to feed them, and . . ."

"Feed them? They didn't need to eat," he said. "They ate this morning."

"But they were hungry!"

"They're always hungry," he said. "Come on, let's get them back in their houses."

"We tried," said Fiona. "But they are kind of bitey. They aren't like Flo!"

Then Tom turned out the lights in the pavilion. The birds suddenly became very still. Tom began to whisper, "Hushabye, hushabye. Hush, hush." He said that over and over again. And as he did, he scooped up the birds one by one and placed them gently in their cages.

"How does he do that?" Cleo whispered to Fiona.

Fiona said, "What he knows about chickens is flat-out a lot."

"I'll say." Cleo looked at the clock. "It's two!"

Fiona scrambled to help Tom with the chickens. "Cleo, go stand watch by the door. And whatever you do, don't let the judges come in until all the chickens are back where they belong."

Cleo raced to the door and yanked it open, and there in front of her were a bunch of people ready to do some chicken judging. "They're here!" hollered Cleo.

"Oh no," said Fiona, ushering a brown hen into a cage and locking the door. There were still chickens everywhere, and she was in such a hurry to get them back in that she didn't make sure they got into the right cages. "Don't let them in yet!"

Fiona started to run toward the door. But the floor was littered with feathers and food, and her feet slipped right out from under her. She landed face-first in a pile of chicken feed.

• Chapter 19 •

The lights came on. And the judges, there were three of them, stood over Fiona. "What has happened in here?" said one woman, swatting at a feather that came floating by her head.

Another woman reached down to Fiona and offered her hand. Fiona grabbed on and got to her feet. "Who is responsible for this mess?"

Tom quickly put the last of the chickens away. Then he stepped forward. "That would be me."

The third judge, a man, said, "We're going to have to notify the owners of these animals right away."

"They aren't hurt," said Tom. He picked a feather out of Fiona's hair. "They just got a little rustled is all. If you give me some time, I can make sure they all get back into their proper cages."

"And we'll help," said Cleo. "Won't we, Fiona?"

Fiona had no words. All she could do was nod after Cleo elbowed her in the ribs.

"Sorry I'm late. Let's judge some chickens," said a young man, who appeared in the doorway with a camera. "Whoa, what happened in here?" He snapped some pictures. The flash on his camera startled a couple of chickens. "I cover the animal beat for *Ordinary News Post*. So, where are we with the judging?" His flash went off again.

"Your camera is bothering the hens," Tom told him.

"Sorry," said the reporter. "No harm, no foul." Then he laughed.

"Fowl!" said the judges, laughing.

"I don't get what's so funny," Fiona said to Cleo.

"Chicken humor, I guess," said Cleo.

"Hold on to your camera," said the man judge. "We haven't gotten to the judging as of yet. We're dealing with something here."

"Now," said the judge to Fiona and Cleo. "Who are you and what are you doing here?"

Cleo told him that she and Fiona went to Ordinary Elementary School and that they had been handing out maps.

"Then I suggest you get back to where you're supposed to be."

Tom looked at Fiona and nodded toward the door. Cleo pulled on Fiona's arm. "Come on, Fiona. Let's go."

Fiona shook her head. What would happen to Tom? He was going to get in trouble because of her. If she didn't say anything.

"Go on now," said the man, looking right at Fiona. Cleo pulled on Fiona's arm again, harder this time. And her feet began to move. "You kids have no business in here."

Maybe it was because she was surrounded by chickens. Or maybe it was because she sucked in too many feathers. But whatever the reason, in that second, Fiona knew what it felt like to really act like a grown-up. It felt like she stepped out of her cage and into a place she'd never been before. She was someplace new, and she didn't know the rules.

The man pointed his finger at Tom. "You better come with me."

"No!" shouted Fiona, climbing on top of the stool. Her feet were heavy, her toes weighed down with sand. "Wait!" And to Fiona's surprise, they did. "It was me, not Tom, that did all of this." She pulled a chicken feather out of her hair and let it fall to the floor. Then she explained what she did and why she did it. "Have you ever heard hungry chickens before?" she asked them. "They are very loud."

The judges just looked at each other. They didn't seem to know how loud hungry chickens could be. So Fiona went on. "And this is Tom. He trains chickens. Or one chicken, anyway."

"Fiona," said Tom. "Stop."

"They should know what you can do," she said. "He is very good with animals, and his chicken, Flo, can walk on a leash. You should see her." She looked at Tom. "They should know what you can do. You're probably going to lose your job because of me, and people should know what you can do."

The reporter snapped a picture of Fiona. "Is that going to be in the paper?" said Cleo. "Maybe you want to take one of me too."

"Fiona Finkelstein and Cleo Button!" Mr. Bland bellowed from the doorway.

"Do these girls belong to you?" said the judge.

"Unfortunately, yes," said Mr. Bland. "You two. Come with me."

Fiona climbed down off the stool. It was over.

• Chapter 20 •

The next day, Fiona sat on the couch with Mr. Funbucket's fishbowl in her lap. "Grown-ups don't get grounded, do they?" she asked Mrs. Miltenberger.

"Nope."

"Good," said Fiona. "Then I hope I get grounded."

"What are you talking about?" said Max. He jumped off the couch and raced around the living room.

Fiona smiled at him. "Want to play later? After I'm done being grounded?"

"You never want to play with me," he said.

"Fine," she said. "You don't have to."

He pulled his swim goggles over his eyes. "Okay, we can play."

Dad called from his study, "Fiona, can you come in here, please?"

Fiona took a deep breath. She set Mr. Funbucket's bowl on the coffee table. "Wish me luck." And then she saw them. "Legs! Mr. Funbucket has legs!"

"Well, what do you know," said Mrs. Miltenberger. "I knew it would happen one of these days. He's on his way to being a frog. Are you happy now?"

Fiona looked closely at his little nubby legs. "It seems like it was only yesterday he was a pollywog without any legs. And now look at him."

Max stuck his head into the bowl. "What are you talking about? It was only yesterday!" Then he took off up the stairs.

"But legs are what you wanted, right?" said Mrs. Miltenberger.

"I thought so," said Fiona. "But he doesn't look like Mr. Funbucket anymore."

Mrs. Miltenberger shook her head. "You are something."

"Fiona!" said Dad. "I'm waiting."

"Better face the music," said Mrs. Miltenberger.

Fiona trudged into her dad's office. "Have a seat," he said.

She sat in the chair in front of his desk. "Sorry, Dad." But he was smiling. "What?"

"I just got off the phone with your mother," he said. "She got a TV commercial. It's not another soap, but it's something. She's happy."

"That's great."

"It also means that she will probably be coming home for a visit soon. So you won't have to keep asking me about going out to California on your own."

"Okay," said Fiona.

"Okay? That's it? After all the talk about you

being old enough to get on a plane and fly across the country alone, that's what you're saying now? Okay?"

"Yep."

"Well, that was easy, then," said Dad.

Fiona got up to go.

"Not so fast."

Fiona slid back into her seat.

"This is the part where you ground me, right?" asked Fiona.

"Afraid so."

"Okay," she said. "Let's have it."

"Okay, then," said Dad. "For two weeks, and no TV."

Fiona smiled. It felt good to be an ordinary fourth grader again. At least the rules made sense.

Dad handed her a section of the *Ordinary News Post* and pointed to a picture. "It's Tom!" said Fiona. "But there's no picture of Flo. I hope she's okay."

"He must really have a way with chickens."

"He does," said Fiona. "His pet chicken is named Flo, and she thinks she's a dog."

"A chicken that thinks she's a dog," said Dad. "That's something you don't see every day."

And that's when Fiona got an idea. "Can I go now and start my grounding tomorrow?"

"Why?"

"I think I know why Flo's been acting so strange," said Fiona.

Fiona found Tom and Flo at the park. "She's just not herself," Tom said. "She doesn't want to go for a walk, and she won't eat."

"Come with me," said Fiona. "I think I know what's wrong."

The trio made their way across town. Mrs. Lordeau was waiting for them on her front porch with Mayflower. "What are we doing here?" said Tom.

"You'll see," said Fiona. "Now put Flo down for a second."

Tom gently put Flo on the grass. She gave a soft cluck and then tucked her head under her wing. "See?" said Tom. "She's just not right."

"Hold on," said Fiona. Then she nodded for Mrs. Lordeau to bring over Mayflower. He bounded off the porch steps, his legs moving as fast as they could go down the sidewalk. He stopped right in front of Flo, sniffed her head, and then nestled in beside her. Flo clucked and flapped her wings. She rubbed her head along Mayflower's back and settled in against him.

"Well, how about that," said Tom.

"Now I've seen everything," said Mrs. Lordeau.

Fiona smiled. "She missed Mayflower! That's why she wasn't acting right!"

Mrs. Lordeau started talking to Tom about chickens and dogs and hardly gave Tom a chance to say much. Which Fiona thought was probably okay with Tom on account of the fact that he thought people were hard to talk to. But Tom nodded and even smiled once when Mrs. Lordeau called him "lovey." And Fiona thought that maybe Tom wouldn't mind some company after all.

Mayflower howled and ran in a circle around Flo. "What are you doing now, boy?" said Mrs. Lordeau.

"I think he wants to go for a walk," said Tom.

Mrs. Lordeau got Mayflower's leash, and they started off toward the park. "Aren't you coming?" Mrs. Lordeau asked Fiona.

"No," she said. "You go ahead."

"You sure?"

She was. As Fiona watched them walk toward

the sunset, her feet began to feel lighter. She had missed this feeling, and it never felt so good. Maybe it had been there all along, and she just never noticed it before.

Fiona stretched her legs. She was glad to be back in her world. And she skipped all the way home.

Life in the White House will never be the same!